To Al and Jo
I really hope you enjoy

Once upon a Grandma

Written and illustrated by

Sarah Helen Harrison

Best wishes from
Sarah

First published in 2009 by
Swanfield, Surrey, England

ISBN 978-0-9561506-0-8

www.onceuponagrandma.com

About the author

Sarah Helen Harrison is an artist, musician and language teacher. She is married with two daughters and lives in Godalming, Surrey.

CONTENTS

Chapter One
A HOUSE OF GREAT AGE 7

Chapter Two
WORSE THINGS HAPPEN AT SEA 17

Chapter Three
GRANDPA IN THE LIMELIGHT 26

Chapter Four
A NOBLE ACT 35

Chapter Five
STAYING UP LATE 45

Chapter Six
SPRING CLEANING 56

Chapter Seven
A RED-LETTER DAY 65

Chapter Eight
IDEAS ABOVE HIS STATION 74

Chapter Nine
IN PRAISE OF RAIN 82

Chapter Ten
THE SECRET PLAN 92

Chapter Eleven
WEDNESDAY THE FIRST 102

Chapter Twelve
JAZZ ON THE LAWN 111

Chapter One
A HOUSE OF GREAT AGE

At home with Grandma – the joys of being spoilt – washing still required in the mornings – the hidden staircase – the grandfather clock – cows and cavaliers

GRANDMA'S house is five hundred years old. It smells of Pears soap and polished wood. Things change in the world outside, but nothing changes here. When I told Grandma one day that my school-friend Rosemary had got a machine to do the washing up, all she could see in her mind's eye was a vision of Grandpa and his dishcloth suddenly automated – which made her laugh so much that she had to sit down and wipe her eyes on her apron.

For a month every summer and a fortnight every spring, Grandma's house is my home. On many an evening we sit in the inglenook, she on her three-legged stool and I on my sawn-off log, one each side of the high copper hood which draws the smoke into the chimney. We talk of this and that, and when there's nothing left to say we are silent, listening to the whispering fire and the clicking of Grandma's knitting needles.

Grandpa leaves his armchair and goes out into the kitchen to make yet another pot of the weakest tea known to man, while Pippy the Dog chases rabbits in his sleep with muffled yips and twitching feet, and the clock ticks slowly in the hall.

I have never been to Grandma's house in the winter. The last time Mum and Dad came here for Christmas, before I was born, they had to scrape ice off the *inside* of the bedroom window and Grandma was quite mortified. Mum says that when she was a girl you expected houses to be freezing cold upstairs, but these days we are all getting softened up, and a good thing too.

I am curious to see the ice on the inside of the windows. I think I would rather like to be here when snow blankets the sleeping fields and logs blaze on the fire all day long, when the milk bottles on the step push their lids into the air, and Grandpa does the washing up in his hat and overcoat and a cloud of steam. But Grandma says I couldn't possibly come at that time of the year: she and Grandpa are used to seeing their breath inside the house, but it's not fit for anyone else. Grandma doesn't often put her foot down, but on the subject of winter visitors she is firm.

It's in the summer that Grandma's house comes into its own, kept cool inside by the thatch and the thickness of the walls. Downstairs the house feels spacious – grand, almost – but upstairs the sloping floors and low attic ceilings make it difficult to fit the furniture in properly, and when you go through the door from Grandma and Grandpa's room into the passage, you have to duck your head and step over the beam that holds the house together. At the other end of the passage is the guest chamber, as Grandma likes to call it, and my white-painted room under the eaves is in between.

I sometimes open my bedroom window wide and reach down to touch the thatch on the roof of the garden porch. It feels hard and dry and slightly crumbling. Once I pulled out a long strand of thatch just to see what it was like: the end was grey with years of weather, but the part that had been hidden was still the colour of fresh straw.

When I wake in the morning in the crisp white bed, higher than my bed at home, I lie still in the deep quiet and let the sunlight glow through my closed eyelids. There's no alarm clock, only a few sparrows cheeping outside the window, and sometimes a distant cock-crow from Sam's farmyard down the lane. Presently other morning sounds begin to drift up from below – Grandpa laying the breakfast table, the eight o'clock pips on the radio, the clock striking a fraction late.

I sit up, reach for my book and turn my pillow on its end. In a few minutes I hear careful footsteps on the stairs, then three taps on the door, and Grandma comes in preceded by a cup of steaming tea with two *Morning Coffee* biscuits in the saucer. They are plain-looking but, as Grandma says, "nicer than they ought to be". I usually dunk them, since dunking is rather frowned upon at home. So is tea in bed, for that matter. Grandma creeps out of the room and back downstairs as if morning tea were some kind of deadly conspiracy; but if I feel a pang of guilt at being waited on I brush it aside, remembering that Grandma is enjoying herself as much as I am.

While I drink my tea I make the bedspread into mountain ranges with my knees. The yard gate clicks open and shut, and I hear Grandma's footsteps setting off down the lane to buy bacon and sausages for breakfast. When the footsteps come back, it's time to get up.

I slide down off the bed straight into my waiting slippers and step across to the window. In spring I can see the roof of Sam's farmhouse and the top of the church tower down in the village, but when the trees along the edge of the orchard are in full leaf, only one other building can be seen from here – Miss Winterton's cottage three fields away to the left. There are several other cottages neighbouring Miss Winterton's, along the bottom road which leads to the Farmer's Arms, but they are hidden by the swell of the fields.

Grandma isn't a great one for paying formal calls, but we do sometimes call on Miss Winterton. She has an electric fire in her inglenook and a cleaning lady who comes every day. I have to wear a frock and sit nicely, but Miss Winterton always makes a great fuss of me, and has

lovely cake. Beyond Miss Winterton's cottage are the hills – a long, low ridge of blue.

I unhook my dressing gown from the back of the door and cross the passage to the bathroom. Grandpa's tooth-mug stands empty on the wash-basin under the window. Over on the sunny side of the yard, Pippy the Dog snoozes in his favourite place against the fence, and far off, to the right of the tall tree by the outhouse, is the wooded knoll where we often take him for a long afternoon walk.

I turn the tap marked "H" with a familiar squeak. Washing is even less inviting at Grandma's than it is at home, because the water is slow to come hot, and too soft to rinse the lather off properly. It's tempting to make do with a quick splash under the running tap, but Grandma always knows.

"Have you washed this morning?"

"Yes!"

"With hot water?"

"Mmm…"

"And soap?"

"We-ell…"

How can she tell? I have never yet fathomed the mystery.

So, with my face *and* neck *and* ears thoroughly flannelled, I make my way backwards on all fours down the steep spiral stairs, which I always think are best treated as a mountaineering exercise. A worn red carpet is nailed down the middle, and the handrail is a thick rope threaded through rings on the wall. The stairs don't creak, in spite of their great age, because each one is carved from a single piece of oak.

At the foot of the staircase, right up against the bottom stair, there is a low door which opens outwards into the room we call the middle room, thinly carpeted and empty of furniture but for Grandpa's grand piano. On the wall above the fireplace hangs a large oil painting of a boy in

white silk trousers and a dark tail-coat, who is supposed to be Grandpa's ancestor. He has tiny hands and even tinier feet, and a canary perched on one finger. The boy appears to be floating an inch or two above the red velvet chair he is sitting on, although I'm sure the artist didn't mean it to look like that. Grandma says it surely must be the worst painting anyone ever thought worth framing in gold, but it's better than a blank wall.

The middle room is rather a forbidding place. When I was younger, I used to like pretending to myself that it was a room in an enormous house where I was a stranger, an orphan who had just arrived to live with a reclusive great-uncle (or sometimes, for variety, a reclusive great-aunt). I would prowl around the room, not noticing the staircase door at first, but squinting through half-closed eyes at the peculiar painting to make it look more like a real boy, and playing quiet snatches of my latest piece on the piano, with too much pedal. Then, catching sight of the small door and murmuring, "I suppose that must be a broom cupboard," I would cross the floor and ever so slowly lift the latch, to discover the mysterious stairs as though for the first time. Once I wrote a note – with my left hand, to make the writing weak and spidery – and slipped it under the stair-carpet for myself to find later. It said, "I am held prisoner in the east wing. Please rescue me before it is too late."

No-one would linger in the middle room unless they wanted to play the piano or dream foolish daydreams – or both. If they were a visitor they would pass swiftly through it into the end room, a respectable and cosy parlour with a thick-pile carpet that goes all the way to the walls, and armchairs drawn up close to a small brick fireplace. In one corner there is an ottoman wedged tightly full of old *Countryman* and *Amateur Gardening* magazines and *Vogue* knitting patterns, and next to the fireplace stands a large glass-fronted bookcase. I often go in the end room by myself to read or draw, and Grandma and I sometimes listen from there when Grandpa plays the piano, because we can't hear it too well from the living room. But mostly the end room is for visitors and special occasions.

Mum and Dad are entertained in the end room when they first arrive to collect me, but after that they go back to being members of the family and helping with the jobs. Other visitors are rare. Some people called Uncle Howard and Auntie Marjorie came to tea once, but whether they were real relations or just old friends of Grandma's I can't remember. Grandma got out the silver teapot and the three-tiered cake stand, and I wore my Sunday best. Uncle Howard was very tall and had a very loud laugh, and gave me a brand new threepenny bit which, to my great astonishment, he had found behind my ear.

Leaving the end room and passing quickly through the middle room again, you come to the hall. The hall is really just a wide passage running from the front of the house to the back. It is closed off at one end by the massive rough-timbered yard door and at the other by the studded door to the garden. The yard door is the one that visitors come to, but I think the garden door must have been the front door once. When the doors are closed the hall is dark as night, but when they are both propped open, a person standing in the yard can see clear through the house to the sunlit garden beyond.

The hall has everything in it that a hall should have: an ancient oak chest full of gardening shoes and badminton racquets, with a row of coat-hooks above; a cluster of umbrellas and walking-sticks in a metal stand; a barometer you can tap; and a grandfather clock whose elegant finial almost grazes the ceiling.

The grandfather clock is a noble presence, grave and distinguished. If I am on my way through the hall just before the hour, especially if it's eleven or twelve, I like to stay for the striking of the clock. Sometimes I open the clock-case door and watch the pendulum; sometimes I lean back among the coats and macks which hang on the hooks above the chest, and hunt through pockets for one of Grandma's folding rain-hats to roll round my fingers while the slow minutes tick by. At the appointed moment the clock is seized with urgent whirrings and windings, and then

the hour chimes quite unexpectedly fast and high. The chime fades as rapidly as it came, but the deep, steady *clunk – tock, clunk – tock* goes on, as if it were not the clock but the walls themselves that made the sound.

The clock once inspired me to write a poem, which I found again a couple of years later and hastily tore up: it was called "The Heartbeat of the House".

Here I must briefly mention something not at all poetic – the small room which opens off the yard porch. Although Grandma's house does have an upstairs bathroom, there is no space in it for a toilet, so we make do with the Lav. The Lav is always cold, except in a heat-wave. There is a terrifying noise when you pull the chain, and if you have the misfortune to be in there when the postman comes you have to keep very quiet. I don't like the Izal paper, but at least it's useful for tracing, and for making the easiest musical instrument in the world, the comb-and-paper.

You go down a step from the hall to the living room. It's an odd thought, but if it hadn't been for the hall doorstep I might never have known this house. When Grandma and Grandpa were looking for a house in the country just after Mum had grown up and left home, this one didn't seem very appealing at first. It was empty and unloved at the time, its barns and byres knocked down and its fields sold off to the farmers round about. Other house-hunters must have thought it too primitive or too far from the village shops, but Grandma felt sorry for it and made Grandpa come and have a look round, and he fell in love with it when he saw this step, worn hollow by generations of passing feet.

There is a reason for the step. Long ago when the house was built, a herd of cows slept in what is now the living room, and the step kept the mess from getting into the rest of the house. We found this out from some experts on old buildings, who wrote to Grandpa a few years ago asking to be shown round. When he told me about it later, I decided to name all the cows after flowers in the usual way – Daisy, Buttercup, Marigold, Primrose and as many more as I could think of – and then Grandpa invented a calf called Forget-me-not who always lingered in the pasture when the others came in for the night. When I asked if the bull

was allowed in the house, Grandpa replied drily that he supposed it could well have been, as the living room was fitted up as a cattle-shed and had no china teacups in it in those days.

The history experts revealed other secrets of the house's past. They said that the end room was once a store-room, which is why it has no inglenook, and the walk-in cupboards on either side of the living room fireplace were meant for smoking bacon and drying corn. Ever since then, we have called them "the bacon cupboard" and "the corn cupboard", even though they contain mostly unhistoric items like the vacuum cleaner and the mop bucket.

According to Mrs Studley at the Post Office Stores, a fleeing cavalier once hid in the bread oven at the back of the main fireplace during the Civil War. Having hidden in there myself a few times, I assume that he must have been a very small cavalier, but it is exciting to think of a troop of roundheads hammering on the studded door and bursting in to search the place.

Before the days of the cavalier, at the time when the cows still lived in the house, there were no stairs. There was just one upstairs room reached by a ladder, and warmed by the presence of the cattle below. The rest of the downstairs was open to the roof and there wasn't even a chimney, just a hole in the thatch for the smoke to find its way through. Now there are three chimneys, and a winding old staircase which once was new, and the thatch lifts itself over the upstairs windows like bushy eyebrows raised in mild surprise.

🕮

It's usually a little after nine o'clock when I sit down to breakfast with Grandpa at the round table in the living room. We just have time for cornflakes with the cream off the top of the milk (it's a bleak day if the milkman has brought only silver-top) before Grandma joins us, bringing with her the sausage, egg and bacon. Grandma's sausages are thinner and tastier than those we have at home. They are dense and peppery, with

almost-burnt crunchy skins. I always eat mine with HP Sauce, which in Grandpa's opinion ruins the flavour. Grilled toast follows: Grandpa spreads his butter very thick.

After the cows had moved out, the inglenook fireplace was built and this room became a kitchen. That was in the days when people roasted meat on spits over the fire, ate it off wooden plates and threw the bones over their shoulders to waiting dogs. Nowadays there is only one waiting dog, and he gets into trouble if he eats his bone on the carpet.

Some time before Grandma and Grandpa came, a new kitchen was made, in a low wing of the house which had been an outbuilding. There used to be a lot more of these outbuildings, which were joined onto the house in a long rectangle called a barton; but the kitchen, the coalhouse, the garage and the outhouse are all that is left of the barton now.

The kitchen is modern inside, in an old-fashioned sort of way. The floor is covered with green lino streaked with a white pattern which I can't stop myself seeing as an enormous flock of emaciated sheep, and the cupboards are made of some sort of artificial dark wood, with doors that have no handles but spring open when you press them. The only ornaments are Grandma's pots of African violets on the window sills, a *Cathedrals of England* calendar curled up by the steam from the kettle and a collection of my drawings, stuck to the wall with sellotape. A black paper witch on a broomstick, which I made at school when I was seven, hangs by a dingy cotton thread from the strip-light on the ceiling and probably always will, revolving slowly to the right, then just as slowly back again.

Grandma never throws anything away. Jars and tins, matchboxes and bottles, shoe boxes and silver foil are always kept because one day they will "come in". Every paper bag is smoothed out and saved; every envelope becomes a shopping list. Anything that can't possibly be used again is either composted or put on the fire.

If I get tired of having nothing but my now slightly pinching school sandals to wear, and am gripped with a sudden desire to make myself a more interesting pair out of cardboard and string, or if I need a supply of lollipop sticks to build a model of Robinson Crusoe's stockade, Grandma

is guaranteed to have the necessary materials. Whenever I ask for a piece of cloth for some project or other, Grandma says, "Well now, let me look," and goes to her chest of drawers in the corn cupboard, stuffed with remnants of cotton, lace and satin, velvet, tweed and corduroy. In the bottom drawer is a heavy tin full of buttons and belt buckles, some of them relics of Grandma's earliest sewing days. When she left school, she was apprenticed to Miss Grayson, a high-class dressmaker, and she still makes all her own clothes and some for Mum and me. However, there is no dressmaking when I am staying here, except perhaps to measure me up or try something half-made on me for size. Grandma says it's no fun being in a house with someone sewing: cloth all over the table, and the floor strewn with pins and ends of thread.

If Grandma has few visitors, it's not because she's unsociable. She has her friends in the village, but they seem to chat over garden gates instead of holding dinner parties, and that suits me very well. I can go home after Easter leaving a half-finished jigsaw puzzle in the end room, and return three months later to find it exactly as I left it – dusted but undisturbed.

Now and again Grandma asks me if I'd like to play with some of the other children in the village, but I'm quite happy as I am. Perhaps I'm the one who's unsociable.

Grandma is always the same, like her house – never agitated, never hurried. However people speak to her, she always answers gently. She is unflustered by spilt drinks and the other kinds of mishap that make mothers cross. She says Mum only gets annoyed because she's busy, and anyway, that's what grandparents are for. I hope I'll be like her when I'm a grandma myself.

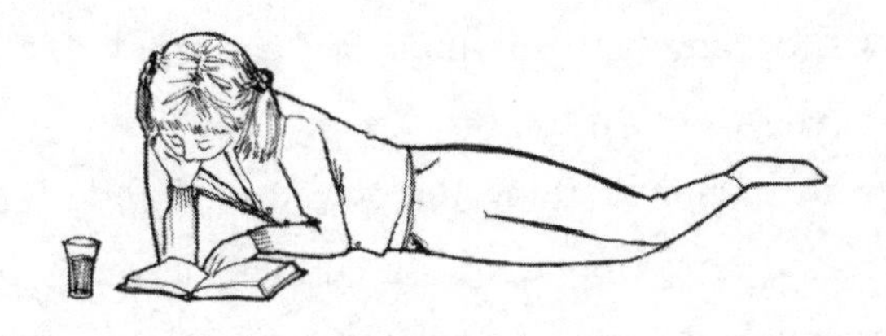

Chapter Two
WORSE THINGS HAPPEN AT SEA

Grandma's annual trip to the beach – contrast with Mum and Dad's seaside holidays – journey into the unknown – a merciful absence of fish – the butter crisis

ONCE every summer at Grandma's, we have a day at the beach. We always wait for a day when the weather is guaranteed to be fine and nobody's favourite television programme is on. Why miss *Casey Jones* if you don't have to?

Our beach is a strip of shingle with an open grassy area at the back, a few bathing huts and a café which closes at five o'clock sharp. I suppose I would prefer it to be an undiscovered cove of golden sand, a former haunt of smugglers overhung by towering cliffs and accessible only at low tide or by boat, but there isn't one of those that we can get to in Lucy the Morris Minor and be back in time for tea.

Grandma's seaside trip is as different as it could be from my annual week at the sea with my parents. Going to the seaside with Mum and Dad means precarious cliff-top walks, adventurous boulder-hopping

along rock-strewn shorelines and splashing in the waves with Mum in her flowery swimming cap while Dad goes snorkelling. It means sailing my wind-up model motorboat in sandy pools left behind by the tide. It means building majestic sand-castles with Dad, carving the ramparts ever steeper with a metal spade, and using pieces of shell and fragments of driftwood to make portcullises, drawbridges and arrow-slits.

Sometimes I borrow Dad's snorkel mask and look through it into a rock pool. I kneel down with my face in the water, so close to the small sheltered world of crabs and sea anemones and fronds of seaweed that I can pretend I am a mermaid who lives down among them.

On wet days we may visit a stately home or a cathedral if there is one, look round some shops or just sit in the car reading. Once we played football on a wide deserted beach, and Mum shockingly tried to cheat by holding onto my anorak to stop me getting the ball. The rain came on heavier so we sheltered in a cave for a while, emerging to draw gigantic faces on the sand.

We go to a different holiday place every year. Sometimes the places we visit have a harbour where you can watch boats, and boys fishing for crabs off the harbour wall with scraps of bacon tied to long pieces of string. One holiday was at a beach with miles of sand-dunes along the back. Another girl and I held jumping competitions, leaping off grassy pinnacles into deep, soft sand, hot on the surface and cold beneath, while our parents read paperback detective stories.

Most seaside places sell sticks of rock with the name of the town printed all the way through them. You peel off the cellophane wrapper and patiently suck the end of the rock into a point. Then you take it home with you and put it in a drawer, where you find it the following year with hairs and fluff stuck to it.

One year we stayed on a farm where there was a real pig in a pigsty. Every morning I went out to the pigsty after breakfast while Mum and Dad were packing up the beach things. I would hang over the stone wall for half an hour watching the vast yet dainty creature snuffling around in

its straw and grunting to itself. It smelt clean and scrubbed, and moved on delicate, two-toed feet. I studied its large hairy ears and tiny eyes. Most fascinating of all was its nose – a pale, flat oval, like a pink plate with a neat pink rim. I hoped it wasn't lonely.

The annual trip to the seaside from Grandma's house is a different thing altogether. There are no cliffs, no pools, no sand, no snorkelling, no rock-eating and no rock-hopping – but I enjoy it just the same. It's a kind of ritual: we drive over the moors, have an early lunch in the car by the roadside, arrive at our stony beach, build piles of shingle, eat ice creams, stare out to sea, paddle in the shallows, contemplate swimming and decide not to bother, have a cream tea in the café and then go home for proper tea.

It's exactly the same every year – except this year.

An observer watching us getting ready would not have forecast any kind of adventure. Everything was just as usual. Lucy the Morris Minor stood waiting in the yard with Pippy settled in on her back seat so he wouldn't have to worry that he might be left behind. Grandma and Grandpa were wearing exactly what they always wear for the beach: Grandma a cotton dress and jacket, white sling-back sandals and a silk headscarf to stop her hair blowing about, Grandpa a linen suit, canvas shoes and a panama hat. Grandma had made some perfectly square sandwiches out of sliced bread and processed cheese, with extra butter on Grandpa's, and Grandpa had brought in some pears from the orchard which felt ominously hard to me. When the picnic basket was packed with the sandwiches, pork pie, hard-boiled eggs, thermos of tea and all, Grandpa slid a block of fruit-and-nut chocolate down the side in the manner of a spy concealing a secret transmitter.

"Better take cardigans," said Grandma. "There could be a nippy breeze off the sea." So I fetched one of mine and one of hers, and then went in search of a tube of sun-tan lotion, so that we should be ready for anything.

The first half-hour of the journey took us on a winding route through the villages, and I knelt on Lucy's back seat watching the receding road. From time to time a dog would run out yapping at the car and chase us for a short distance, and Pippy would scratch his way up the seat back and bark threateningly through the rear windscreen. Once we were away from the lanes and on the main road to the coast, Grandpa speeded up to a breathtaking forty miles per hour, and I settled down with my legs stretched out along the seat to re-read my *Princess Tina Annual for 1971*. Pippy trampled on my feet and made wet nose-marks on the window. Every so often Lucy would shake as another car overtook us on a straight stretch of road. At some point I closed my Annual to start a game of "I Spy," and by the time we had spied with our little eye just about everything inside the car and out of it, including "P.C. Pippy's Collar", "P.T. Pippy's Tail" and "P.N. Pippy's Nose", the moor began rising on one side of us. The owner of the collar, tail and nose thought this scenery looked promising, and stood up with his paws on the side window.

We stopped in our usual lay-by. I let Pippy out onto the grass and tied him to a fence post to eat his own packed lunch while we had our picnic. Grandpa cleaned a smattering of poor squashed flying insects off Lucy's windscreen so that we could enjoy the view.

Now, Mum and Dad would never eat a picnic in the car unless it was raining, and if they did have to eat in the car they would drive for miles along country lanes looking for the perfect field gateway to stop in, rather than just parking in a lay-by on the main road, but as I have said, you do things differently with grandparents – that's the fun of it.

As soon as we had eaten our sandwiches, eggs and pork pie, and Grandma had gnawed her way through a pear and told us they weren't worth eating, I ran straight up over the shoulder of the hill onto the moor with Pippy. Grandma and Grandpa followed more slowly by the track, bringing the chocolate and the flask of tea with them.

Up here was a wide and glorious view. I could see the sea, and smell fresh air, early blackberries and bracken. Scattered about everywhere were enormous rocks patterned with grey and green lichen. I climbed on and

off them and hid in hollows underneath while Pippy conducted explorations of his own. For him this was the best part of the day. He was his happiest self on the moor, putting his nose into interesting-looking holes, burrowing into thickets and coming out again backwards, then standing still and panting with his head up into the wind, as if posing for a photograph. I fell about this way and that among the springy heather and bracken, making regular trips to the rock where Grandma and Grandpa leaned comfortably sipping tea and dispensing soft squares of chocolate. Grandma's headscarf rippled in the breeze. It was some time before we were ready to go back to the car.

After a few more miles of road with only glimpses of the sea, once again it lay in full view before us. Lucy crunched over the gravel of the beach car park and I jumped out to put ten new pence into the honesty box. "It was a shilling last year," said Grandpa. "They all double their prices and think we won't notice."

The beach was lightly sprinkled with groups of people. We stumbled along over the stones, carrying Pippy, until we were out of earshot of someone's transistor radio. Having chosen a good spot, we spread our tartan rugs lumpily over the shingle. Grandpa got out his book and Grandma her knitting, and they made themselves as comfortable as could be managed. Grandpa kept hold of Pippy's lead in case any other dogs should pass by, and I began collecting some of the largest, flattest stones to build a tower with.

Pippy, restless at first, had just dozed off with his head on Grandma's foot when raucous chimes behind us announced the arrival of the ice cream van. My tower of stones having suffered its inevitable collapse at the same moment, Grandma and I made our way to the back of the beach and across the grass to buy a block of Cornish in wafers for Grandpa and three cones. Pippy used to finish Grandma's ice cream for her, but now he has his own *and* finishes Grandma's – a glaring example of what Grandpa calls "gaining the Upper Paw."

I gazed loftily out to sea and licked round and round my ice cream, making sure there was some left to eat with the very last bit of cone.

Down by the shore a temporary jetty on wheels had been drawn up. There was a sign board placed there and half a dozen people were gathered round in a sort of untidy queue. I shaded my eyes with my hand and watched as a small boat made its way down from the horizon. Eventually it reached the jetty, and the people began getting on. This was something new.

"Look, Grandma," I said, "those people are going on a boat trip."

"Oh, yes," said Grandma, more interested in her knitting.

"Couldn't *we* go?" I persisted. "We might get a really nice view of the bay. It'd be fun for a change."

"Go on," said Grandpa. "The dog and I can look after the gear."

"All right then. Why be boring?" Grandma put her needles together, stuck the ball of wool on the end and hauled herself up. Grandpa laid down *Mutiny on the Bounty* in order to keep a tight hold on Pippy.

The boat was already being untied from the jetty, so I took Grandma's hand and slightly dragged her along, carrying her handbag for her. She couldn't run over the shingle in her sandals, and we leapt on board only just in time. The boy with the rope grabbed us by the arms and said, "Mind out there, ladies!" which gave me a grown-up feeling.

"Made it!" I beamed, as we sat down and looked about us. The seven other passengers were all men and boys, which seemed a little unusual. The wiry, stubble-faced captain wore a rakish black cap and a cigarette stuck to his lip, and the boy, who was now talking to him in the cabin as he started the engine, was rather oddly kitted out in shorts and a woolly hat – nothing else. The boat was scruffy for a pleasure craft, and smelt of fish; there was even an untidy pile of fishing tackle on the floor. "Never mind," I thought as I looked back at the churning wake, "it's still nice to be out on the water," – but Grandma was putting two and two together. As the boy came out of the cabin and started taking everyone's money, she leaned over towards me.

"I think we're on a fishing trip," she murmured in my ear.

"*What?*" I hissed. "Why didn't they tell us?"

"I suppose they thought we knew."

Alas, Grandma was right. This was not a sightseeing trip round the bay. Having collected all the money, the boy bent down, picked up the mess of rods and lines from the bottom of the boat and began untangling them to hand out to the passengers. He gave me a funny look when I shrank away with a muttered "No, thank you." Grandma was staring up at a noisy trio of seagulls circling the boat, and the boy failed to attract her attention.

The captain dropped anchor and our companions began rigging their rods and getting into position for fishing. Several more seagulls joined us. Grandma had turned her back on everyone while she struggled not to laugh, but I shut my eyes, full of dread. I enjoy fishing for minnows with a net as much as the next person, but this was different. At any moment, full-sized glittering scaly fish would be flying into the boat and flapping about our feet. It was hard to decide who it was going to be worse for, them or me. I considered jumping over the side and swimming to shore, but it was too far – Grandpa and Pippy and all the other sensible people who had stayed on the beach were dots in the distance. There was nothing for it but to curl up into a ball and await the worst.

Well, we sat and sat, and waited and waited, and nothing happened. The longest half-hour in the history of the world passed, and the boat bobbed up and down a good deal, but no fish flew in or flapped. The seagulls left, having better things to do with their time. The only sounds now were puzzled remarks from the fishermen.

"Not a single bite. What's the matter with 'em?" they began asking. I uncurled myself and saw that Grandma's shoulders were shaking again, and her eyes were closed very tight.

"I dunno – they were like grass yesterday," drawled the captain, scratching his head and furrowing his already-furrowed brow; but the cabin boy shrugged as if it was just the way of the world. The cigarette stayed stuck to the captain's lip while he talked. "Are you ladies sure you don't want any tackle?"

It came as a shock to have our existence noticed once again. "Yes, quite sure, thank you," I croaked, seeing that Grandma was incapable of speech.

We sat on that dreary horizon nearly an hour altogether, and not one fish was caught. Grandma and I couldn't talk to each other, knowing that fishermen prefer silence, so we kept busy with our own thoughts, and grim enough mine were.

The captain pulled up the anchor and moved the boat to a different spot, but there seemed to be no fish in that piece of sea either. Everyone agreed to give up and return to shore, and I nodded the hardest.

When we got back to the beach I jumped out of the boat before anyone else, thanking the captain with a wan smile as he handed me off. I left Grandma behind and strode over to look at the sign board on the jetty, which I had previously been in too much of a hurry to read.

"FISHING TRIPS ON SAUCY SUE," it said. "2 HOURS OR ALL NITE."

At four o'clock we were in the beach café having our usual cream tea. Pippy the Dog was in the car. A whiff of fishing boat lingered about our clothes, and Grandma was still wiping the laughter from her eyes and wondering what the fishing party must have thought of us, while I picked the raisins out of my scones and Grandpa made the distressing discovery that there was no butter.

"Well, that's a fine thing!" He was incredulous at first, and even looked under the table to see if it had dropped onto the floor. "Well, dash it all!" he said, when he was sure that there really was none. He put on his best "speaking to strangers" face and called the waitress across. She replied airily that they didn't serve butter with cream teas.

"We have a cream tea here every year, and there's always butter with it," replied Grandpa, trying his best to remain calm. The waitress gave the opinion that nobody wanted butter as well as clotted cream, and Grandpa replied in a strangled voice that *he* did, and would she please bring him some.

“Always cheerful!” sighed Grandma, squeezing Grandpa’s arm as the waitress flounced off to the kitchen. He began to laugh weakly in spite of himself.

“Grandma,” I asked, “what did the man mean when he said that the fish were like grass yesterday?”

“I suppose he meant there were an awful lot of them – like grass in a lawn.”

I shivered. “Golly!”

“Aren’t we a pair of silly muffins?” said Grandma.

It was gallant of her to share the blame, but there you are, that’s Grandma all over.

Chapter Three
GRANDPA IN THE LIMELIGHT

Two gardens, one gardener – eccentricities of Grandpa – his haircut – discovery of the well bucket – winding the clock – the bonfire

I WENT to bed rather crestfallen that night and planned to spend the next few days in quiet contemplation, repenting for ever of all rashness and bossiness. But by the next morning I was my usual breezy self again, and was clattering round the yard on Mum's old roller-skates pretending to be a beautiful Russian ice dancer when a horse and rider passed by the gate. Fortunately, Pippy wasn't there to make a fuss. Finding my roller-skating unrestful, he had left his sun-bathing place by the fence and gone into the house to continue his snooze in peace.

Grandma was busy with her chores, and Grandpa was round by his shed at the back of the house loading extra tools into his wheelbarrow to take to the allotment. Knowing that he likes a bit of horse manure for his compost heaps, I skated into the outhouse and reached for the shovel. Then, holding onto the gatepost, I launched myself into the lane in order

to collect anything the horse might kindly have left behind. For the greatest efficiency I should have removed the skates, but they were fixed to my lace-up shoes with screws as well as straps and difficult to take off quickly - so I just jammed one skate into a pothole to stop myself rolling down the lane.

I returned triumphantly into the yard just in time to empty the shovel into Grandpa's passing wheelbarrow. "Thank you very much!" said he. "I'll put it straight on the heap down at the garden." And off he went with a spring in his step.

By "the garden" he meant his allotment. Whenever Grandpa is "*in* the garden" he is in the garden behind the house, but if he is "*down at* the garden" he is at the far end of the village among his beloved rasps and rhubarb.

Grandpa likes gardening in the traditional way. He complains that modern gardening is more like chemistry, all sprays and powders. It's one of the things he worries about, along with farmers setting fire to fields of stubble in the autumn, and digging out hedgerows to make their fields ever larger. He can't understand why no-one else seems to think these things are wrong. Grandma says, "Never mind, it can't be helped. Don't get yourself upset," but he still does.

Almost every day after breakfast is washed up, unless it's raining hard, he puts on his flat cap or some other piece of ancient headgear, fetches his barrow round from the back of the house and sets off. He comes home again at about half past twelve, when it's time to bring Grandma the vegetables she needs for mid-day dinner.

That particular morning, he had been gone about an hour when Grandma remembered that she had meant to ask him for a marrow. Would I go and tell him? I had had enough of skating by that time, and was sitting on the step with Pippy next to me.

"Can I go on your bike?"

"If you like. Stop at the corner in case a car comes."

"I will. You stay, Pippy. Not for dogs."

Grandma came and picked Pippy up and took him into the kitchen while I went into the outhouse again, this time to pull out Grandma's heavy old black bicycle. I love Grandma's bike, especially now I can reach the pedals at their lowest point. It has a gear-lever on one handle-bar, which I leave well alone, a bell on the other and a wicker basket fixed to the front which creaks companionably as I ride along.

It was a blissful ride to Grandpa's allotment that sunny morning – gently downhill all the way. The wind lightly lifted my hair, and the only sound was the freewheeling bicycle's *tick-a-tick-a-tick*, accompanied by the occasional sighing of the brakes. Once I was past the awkward corner by the farm gate where I had to get off to check for traffic, I felt bold enough to let the bicycle pick up its own speed. Old Tom, sitting in his usual place outside the Post Office Stores, raised his walking stick in greeting as I sailed by, and I tried to wave back but wobbled dangerously. Opposite the end of Water Lane I braked hard, skidded round into the gravel path that leads to the allotments and half jumped, half fell off the bike.

The allotments are made out of a large field divided into strips, each with its own tidy rows of lettuces and radishes and soft fruit bushes, ranks of tall crossed canes supporting sweet peas or runner beans, and straight grass paths separating the gardens. The only exception to this impeccable neatness is the allotment belonging to a certain Ted Dredge, whose neglected plot is a source of irritation to all the other gardeners, not only because it looks a mess, but also because Ted Dredge's weed seeds blow all over everyone else's patch.

"Odd sort of cove, that fellow Dredge," says Grandpa. Generally he refers to friends and acquaintances (whatever their age) as "*Old* So-and-so", as in "Old Coker," or "Old Tomlinson". To be known as plain "Dredge" is a mark of extreme disfavour.

Each allotment has a wooden shed at one end, and all the sheds are different shapes and sizes. Grandpa's is just big enough to walk into – rather like a sentry-box with a door on. His tools hang from hooks on the walls, and each hook has the shape of the tool that belongs on it

neatly painted on the wall in black, so that when a tool isn't there it's easy to see what's missing. Above the hooks is a shelf holding various odds and ends including some tidy stacks of different-sized plant pots and a row of rusty biscuit tins. Each tin is labelled with its contents: "String", "Pegs", "Plant Tags" and so on.

The largest item in the shed is Grandpa's magnificent canopied deck chair, which he takes out and unfolds before he starts work. It always reminds me of those seats elephants carry on their backs. When he gets tired of digging he sits down in it to plan what to do next. Sometimes if the sun is very warm he dozes off; sometimes another gardener comes across for a chat; but today when I first caught sight of him Grandpa was just sitting quietly thinking, while a robin hopped about on the part of the garden he had been hoeing.

Grandpa is happy enough talking to the other allotment-holders, and I am sure he chats pleasantly to people at the hall where he and Grandma go Old Time Dancing on Friday evenings when I'm not here, but he is generally rather shy and serious in public. People who don't know him would be surprised to hear him reminiscing about the jolly times he used to have as a boy with his elder brothers and cousins, engaging in daring exploits such as hiding whoopee cushions in the chairs of unsuspecting maiden aunts.

Grandpa reads aloud better than anyone I know. He makes up his own stories, too, and enjoys inventing names for things. He calls a weathervane a "windblibber", and the thin little black thunder-flies, that suddenly appear in the garden one week and are gone the next, are "inglimopsids". He is also good at putting on accents. Sometimes, in mid-conversation, he will suddenly take on the role of some imaginary family retainer – Lurch the chauffeur perhaps, Glyde the butler or the easily-shocked governess Miss Perkins, who may at any moment open her eyes very wide at you and trumpet disapprovingly, "A-*pooh*, child!"

Grandpa is very courteous. He always raises his hat and says "I beg your pardon" if he bumps into someone in the street or gets in their way by mistake. He can be irritable sometimes, complaining about "blighters"

who dump rubbish in the lane, or "idiots" who roar through the village on motorbikes on Saturday nights. But he usually ends up laughing at himself, with or without Grandma's help.

When he isn't down at the garden he is often found in the greenhouse, fiddling with tomato plants and listening to the Third Programme on the wireless, as he calls it, his trousers hitched up to a pair of striped braces. One day in the greenhouse he felt a tickle on his head and took off his hat to find a spider inside it making a web. Not wanting to disturb it, he went back into the house, hung up the hat very carefully and took another one. He is less tolerant of flies, however – unlike Grandma who thinks they should be ushered out politely rather than being swatted. Once, he became so engrossed in trying to swat a fly which was crawling about on the inside of Lucy's windscreen that he ran gently into the car in front.

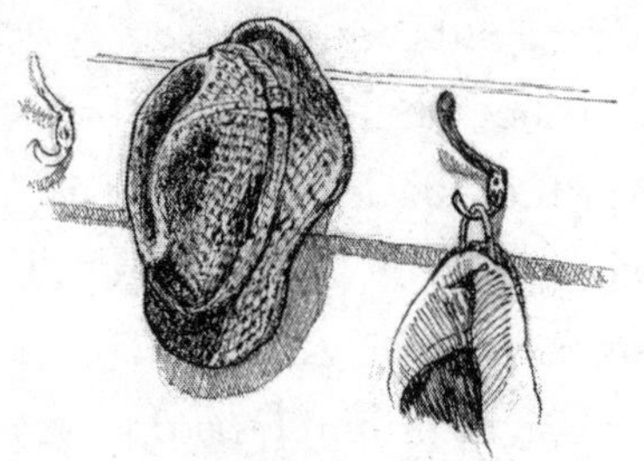

📖

I waved to Grandpa from the entrance to the allotments, but he was deep in thought in his regal deckchair. I left the bike against the hedge and walked along the main grass path with my arms out as though it was a tightrope. Various digging men looked up as I passed and nodded "Good morning."

Drawing level with the deckchair I cleared my throat slightly so as not to make Grandpa jump, and told him that a marrow was required. He stood up and touched his cap in a suitably deferential manner.

"Anything for her ladyship," said he, putting on his "Bindweed the gardener" voice and reaching into his pocket for the worn bone-handled knife he always uses to cut vegetables. "Would you like to dig up some potatoes, young Missie?"

"Oh yes, Bindweed, I like doing that."

Driving the fork in underneath the potato plant, I levered it up until the roots were exposed. I crumbled off the dry clods of pinkish-brown earth with my other hand, and there were the small waxy potatoes, some

dropping off onto the soil and some clinging to the roots. I collected them into a black rubber bucket and threw the rest of the plant onto Grandpa's compost heap. Then there were carrots to pull and peas to pick. It needed perseverance to find the long green pea pods: each time I was sure I had picked them all, there was always one more, hiding itself among the sun-striped leaves.

Mr Bindweed tugged at his cap again. "Would you like to take they peas home and shell 'em, young Missie? Please be so good as to tell her ladyship I'll bring the rest of the veg in the wheelbarrow when I comes." I held open a string bag for him to drop the pea pods into, and he gave me a rag to wipe my hands on.

"Thank you, Bindweed. Don't be late."

"Not I, young Missie."

I carried the bag of peas to the edge of the allotments and settled it into the bicycle basket. Then I pushed the bike slowly home.

🕮

After lunch it was announced by Grandma without any previous warning that the time for Grandpa's haircut had come.

Now, the top of Grandpa's head is completely bald: he calls it his parting. But round the sides there is plenty of greyish-white hair which curls at the ends when it begins to grow long. Haircut day arrives abruptly whenever Grandma thinks the curls are becoming too luxuriant.

Grandpa didn't argue, but meekly went to fetch a towel. He seated himself backwards on a kitchen chair, with his arms on the chair back and the towel round his shoulders, while Grandma got out her sewing scissors. Then he gazed stoically at the ceiling as one lock after another spiralled to the floor. Within five minutes they were all gone.

At this point you might have thought the job was finished, but the hairdresser was not satisfied. Firmly she tilted Grandpa's head forward and shaved up the back of his neck with an alarming-looking instrument like a miniature lawn-mower.

"That's better," said Grandma, when only a narrow fringe of short white hair was left. She walked all round him twice, eyeing the results critically. "All right, you can go now."

"Ooh, it's draughty," shuddered the victim, turning his shirt collar up. "Is my parting straight?" He escaped to go and look for a scarf, while Grandma swept up the curls from the floor.

Later that afternoon, still wearing his paisley-patterned silk scarf, Grandpa got out the full-sized lawn-mower, and Pippy and I helped him cut the grass – by which I mean that we watched from the garden seat, getting off and helping him to move it when it was time to mow underneath. This is an example of what Grandpa calls "being pally".

You can't really plan being pally – it just happens sometimes: like the day when Grandpa, about to put away the lawn-mower after mowing the lawn, decided instead to make a see-saw by balancing a ladder on the upturned grass-box. He sat at one end and I sat at the other and we went up and down, but of course his feet never left the ground. Or there was the evening – one of those evenings full of the left-over warmth of a long, hot day – when Grandpa found a book of easy piano duets, and we played them over and over with the window wide open while Grandma knelt on the path just outside, pulling up weeds from between the stones and applauding us at polite intervals.

When I was about five, and staying here with Mum, Grandpa told me that he had been poking around in the roof of the outhouse, in a dark corner which even he had never before felt inspired to clear out, and had made an exciting discovery. It was something old, belonging to the house, which everyone had always thought was lost, and he had very nearly given it to the rag-and-bone man, not realising at first what it was. He beckoned to me to follow him into the back garden. There by the well stood a battered-looking metal object, something like a milk churn, but wider in the middle than at the top and bottom. Grandpa sat down on the edge of the well with the object on his knee, leaned over and looked significantly down into the well shaft, and then I realised what the thing was. It was the old original well bucket, and it had that shape to

prevent water spilling out of it as it swung its way up from the bottom of the well.

There had been a hole in the bucket, which Grandpa had arranged to have mended. He had taken away the other bucket, the ordinary one he had put in the well years before because Mum said there ought to be one, but he had waited for my arrival before attaching its replacement.

I held the bucket handle up so that he could tie it onto the rope, while Grandma watched and Mum took some photographs. Then we lifted the hinged wooden well-cover and turned the handle to let the bucket down until it landed with a far-away splash in the depths of the well. When it had had time to fill, we wound it slowly back up, and Grandpa helped me tip the cold, clear water into a watering can and pour it on the herbaceous border, while Mum took more photographs.

The bucket has stayed in its place on the well ever since, and is still used to water the garden in dry weather.

Sometimes I help Grandpa wind the grandfather clock in the evening. I open the tall narrow door in the front of the clock-case so that I can see the weights hanging down on their chains behind the pendulum. One weight works the clock, the other the chime. Grandpa reaches for the key which lives on top of the clock, and I stand on a chair and put the key into one of the two holes in the clock face. It doesn't really look like a key – it's just a bent metal rod with a revolving wooden knob on the end to hold it by. As I turn it, one of the weights slowly rises to the top of the case. Then I put the key into the other hole and wind up the second weight. Finally I step down off my chair and close the case door, while Grandpa replaces the key in its high hiding place.

Perhaps the palliest activity of all is tending the bonfire together. The heap in the orchard gradually builds up with garden prunings and any

stalks from the allotment which are too tough to compost, and when the heap grows high enough and a suitably windless evening comes along, Grandpa heads out to the orchard at dusk with a box of matches and a fork. Sometimes I don't know he's gone until I see the smoke rising from behind the beech hedge, and then I run out to join him. I pick up stray twigs and throw them onto the fire, and if I find any good-sized sticks I poke them in and light the ends, and wave them around like sparklers on November the Fifth, while Grandpa leans on his fork and gives a little grin. Our faces glow in the firelight, and the sparks fly upwards into the dark.

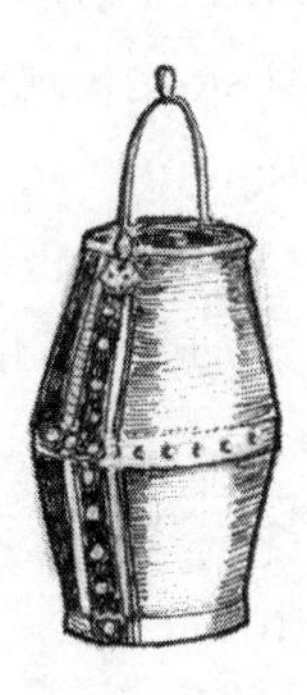

Chapter Four
A NOBLE ACT

A long-felt want – suspicious behaviour of some grown-ups – the Post Office Stores – Grandma shown to have no talent for espionage – a momentous event

PIPPY is my dog, but he lives with Grandma. He wasn't always here – he arrived quite unexpectedly five years ago, the year I was eight.

Grandma knew I had always wanted a dog. I wasn't particular – any kind of dog would do, as long as it was small enough to pick up and not too hairy. I had pestered Mum and Dad about it for ages, and they were very apologetic, but they didn't think they wanted an animal to look after for years on end. I tried to make it a bit easier by suggesting we could get an oldish dog from a dogs' home, but they replied that an oldish dog might have bad habits, and in any case, even a well-trained non-hairy dog with immaculate self-grooming skills would still be a tie and stop us going abroad. I pointed out that we never went abroad, and if we did the dog could go in kennels, but Mum said she didn't like the idea of kennels,

which seemed to me a feeble reply. Dad asked why I never played with other people's dogs, and I said I didn't know – a dog of my own would be different. I suppose that seemed a pretty feeble reply to *him*.

So it went on: they never actually said *No*, but they never did say *Yes*, either. Then Mum got her job, and that really was the end of it, as it seemed.

Grandma told me she quite understood how Mum and Dad felt. A dog did tie you down, there was no denying it. It needed company. It wanted a walk every day, whatever the weather, and someone had to feed it and clean up after it. Dogs came into houses with muddy paws and gritty coats and generally failed to understand the purpose of door mats: some – heaven forbid! – even wiped dirt onto walls with their tails. Training them was hard work. Even the most ardent dog-lover would probably admit that dogs have their drawbacks.

I understood all that, but I needed a dog, all the same.

"I'll just have to wait until I'm grown-up," I thought. "Then I'll live on a house-boat with a dog of my own. I'll just have to be patient."

While I waited to be grown-up I made do with an imaginary dog called Scamp, who lived under my bed. I drew endless pictures of Scamp, took him for pretend walks and trained him with no difficulty at all to walk on his hind legs and jump through hoops.

Then, the year I was eight, Grandma and Grandpa did a heroic thing.

I arrived at Grandma's that summer with no inkling of what was planned. Mum came with me on the train, as she always did in those days, and stayed the night. On the day we arrived all seemed normal, apart from the weather, which was most unseasonably grey, damp and cold. After lunch Grandpa lit the fire in the end room, and while the grown-ups talked I did what I always do on my first day at

Grandma's: I knelt down in front of the bookcase next to the fireplace, opened the glass doors with the tiny gold key and drew in the familiar dry smell of old closed-away books.

Many of the books in Grandma's bookcase have dark red covers, with mysterious gold-lettered titles such as *I Will Repay*, *The Man in the Iron Mask*, or *The Murder of Roger Ackroyd*. Taking up almost a whole shelf is a complete and matching set of the works of Charles Dickens in microscopically small print, with padded leather bindings and gilt-edged pages. Then there are the children's stories – *Our Friend Jim*, *The Violet Bradby Omnibus* and all the others like them – whose tattered dustcovers I long to take off and throw away, but Mum says I mustn't. The characters in them have old-fashioned names such as Maud, Betty, Dick, or Ralph, and say things like "Oh, Mother, how absolutely topping!" and "I say, what rot!" There are cross-hatched drawings of boys in jackets and breeches wearing hats shaped like flower-pots, and girls with ringlets and pom-pom hats, pinafore dresses and black stockings. Some of the books even have colour plates on glossy paper, with captions in small capital letters such as "ALEC WAS THE FIRST TO SEE THE LARGE HOLE". I don't know why, but colour plates are never anywhere near the part of the book they illustrate.

Most of these stories have the pleasing theme of children outwitting grown-ups who are up to no good. I chose one of my favourites, *The Riddle of Gull Cove*, in which four children whose parents have gone to India without them are sent to stay with an elderly aunt by the sea and thwart the schemes of a gang of ruthless criminals. I was soon so lost in the book that I didn't notice Grandma and Mum leave the room, but when they returned their manner seemed furtive, as if they had been talking about something and had to stop just before they came in.

Grandma doesn't normally have secrets from me, and has certainly never been known to plot evil doings, yet at breakfast the following morning I definitely saw her give Mum a significant look, the sort the villains gave each other a lot of in *The Riddle of Gull Cove*. Since, like the enterprising children in the story, I prefer to work things out for myself

rather than asking awkward questions, I narrowed my eyes suspiciously and went outside to think.

The chilly rain of the previous day seemed unreal now. Everything looked fresh and clean in the morning sun: the crazy-paved path with small-leaved plants shooting up here and there between the stones; the bees droning in the lavender that grows round the well; the bench where Grandma and I have our elevenses, gazing out across the garden and the fields and squinting upwards every so often to try to see the larks. We can hear them singing, but they are so high in the sky they are nearly always out of sight.

I looked over the orchard gate and saw that Grandpa had strung up the hammock in its usual place between two of the apple trees.

The orchard is quite small. It's just a triangular grassy patch dotted with a few fruit trees – apples, pears and, far superior to the others in my eyes, a Victoria plum. In one corner is the bonfire place, in another are Grandpa's compost heaps, and in the third corner is the back gate which opens into the lane.

I hooked one leg into the hammock and then rolled the rest of myself in as slowly as I could so as not to fall straight out again on the other side. After much fidgeting to achieve just the right balance, I lay there in dappled sunlight, listening to Sam's tractor somewhere far away and thinking hard, while the hammock gradually became still. Every so often I would move to set it rocking again but, rocking or still, there was no solving the mystery.

Perhaps there was no mystery after all. It couldn't have anything to do with Mum, at any rate, because after a perfectly normal lunch free of conspiratorial behaviour she kissed us goodbye and left for home. But while Grandpa was taking Mum to the station, Grandma reawakened my suspicions by sending me to the Post Office Stores with an empty lemon barley water bottle, my weekly sweet ration which in those days was a shilling, and half-a-crown with which to buy myself some extra holiday treats. Was it my imagination, or was this a plot to get me out of the house?

Summoned by the bell on the door, Mrs Studley appeared from the back of the Post Office Stores in her flower-patterned overall, leaving the curtain of blue, green and white plastic strips swinging behind her. "Hello, my love," she said, without the least surprise in her voice.

Mrs Studley and I don't have big hellos and goodbyes. When I appear at the beginning of each holiday we just take up again where we left off last time. She always knows the sweets I want: whatever quantity my money will buy of red liquorice shoelaces, sherbet lemons, jelly babies, Everton mints and pink candy shrimps, with one or two extra popped in for luck. She tips the sweets out of giant glass jars, stretching her hand to screw the huge lids on and off. The lids are red: they almost match her nail varnish. She weighs each kind of sweet separately, but they all go into one large paper bag, which she then takes by the corners and tosses over and over until it is securely enough closed.

While Mrs Studley was weighing out the sweets, I was jingling my money and studying the available comics, magazines, notebooks, felt pens and coloured pencils, packets of Jaffa Cakes and custard creams, model farm animals, plastic boomerangs, rolls of sellotape and sparkly purses with snap fasteners. After long deliberation, I picked out the latest *Beano,* a bottle of pink nail polish, a sheepdog with three sheep and a length of bendy plastic fence, a black biro, a pack of thin felt pens and a red Silvine exercise book in which to write my usual summer collection of unfinished stories.

"You keep on writing and you'll be a real authoress some day," said Mrs Studley, putting the sweet bag and all my extra purchases into an even bigger paper bag. "There you are, my love. And here's Grandma's thruppence back on the empty bottle."

The till drawer pinged, the bell on the shop door jangled, and I was off with a "Goodbye, Mrs Studley – see you soon!" As usual I resolved that my sweets would last all week, and as usual by tea time there were just two liquorice shoelaces and a few sherbet lemons left in the bottom of the bag. I knew there would be no more until next week. Grandma does take delight in spoiling me, but she has to have *some* rules.

"What will your mother think if I send you home with bad teeth from eating too many sweets?" she'll say; or of course it might be a pasty face from staying indoors too much, or dark circles under the eyes from staying up too late, or square eyes from watching too much television, or, the worst possibility of all, *looking thin.*

That evening, after a slap-up tea guaranteed to prevent loss of weight, I sat on the round pouffe in the living room, sucking one more sherbet lemon. It had just got to that exciting stage where a sharp-edged hole forms in one end and the sherbet shoots out, making your eyes water. My nails were satin pink and only one was badly smudged. The fire wasn't lit, but Grandma had piled the grate up with logs and fir cones and was very pleased with its artistic appearance.

I undid my pigtails to make them into plaits, and watched Grandma knitting in her armchair. By the time both plaits were finished, she still had not caught my eye once. I looked across at Grandpa reading, and knew by the way his mouth twitched that he was only pretending to read. Something was definitely afoot.

"Would you like a sherbet lemon, Grandma?"

"Oh, goodness, don't start me on those. I'll never be able to stop."

I offered the bag to Grandpa. "No, thank you," he said, looking up from *The Hound of the Baskervilles* and adding, predictably, "They get in your mouth, you know."

There was a slight pause, and then Grandma gave a little "*Ahem*," with her eyes still on her knitting, followed by another longer pause.

"Last Thursday," she began at last, rather casually, "Grandpa and I went along to a place the other side of town. I *think* it was Thursday – or was it Friday? Anyway, as I say, we went to this place we'd heard about – it was just an idea we had. It's called Pampered Pup Kennels. Someone told me they sometimes have dogs there needing homes, so we thought we'd just ask." I sat bolt upright, my sherbet lemon suspended in mid-suck. Grandma put her head on one side and slid the stitches along her needle to even them up. "We thought perhaps we could have a dog here,

you see. It could be your dog, but live with us. Then your Mum and Dad wouldn't have to be bothered with it."

"Oh, Grandma!" I jumped up and threw my arms round her neck, draping myself over the side of her chair. "I knew you were up to something. You wouldn't make a very good spy, you know."

"That's why I married her," said Grandpa, who had put his book down and was leaning back in his armchair with his spectacles still on the end of his nose. I put my head on Grandma's shoulder and accidentally swallowed my sherbet lemon.

Grandma laid her knitting in her lap and patted my arm. "It just so happens," she said, "there *was* a stray dog there – a Jack Russell terrier. He looked a nice little dog. He's still there – I rang up to check today while you were at the Stores. He might be suitable, I don't know. He's been there ages and no-one's claimed him."

"Gosh! What's he like? What's his name?" I sat down cross-legged on the floor in front of Grandma's chair, the way we used to listen to a story at infant school, and ignored the sherbet lemon as it made its way down.

"Well, as he was a stray and had no tag on his collar they didn't know his name, so they called him Pip, after Philip, the man who owns the kennels. He seems very good-natured. He's a bit fat, but I suppose he doesn't get much exercise there."

"Oh, let's rescue him! I expect he's quite old, is he?"

"Not all that old. Their vet thinks he's about four. We could go and see him tomorrow, if you like. But see what you think of him. Don't set your heart on him yet."

"I already have!"

🕮

Next morning I was up and dressed very early, anxious that someone else might even now get there before us, but I still wasn't up as early as Grandpa. He had found a cardboard box lid and an old blanket, and had made quite an inviting-looking bed under the settle in the living room. The settle is so hard and narrow that hardly anyone ever sits on it – its

main function is to keep out the draught from the kitchen. A dog's bed would be warm underneath there and not get in the way.

Breakfast was a quick cornflake, not Grandma's usual fry-up, and in a remarkably short time we were on our way to town in Lucy, with me in the passenger seat encouraging Grandpa in his efforts to put on some speed, and Grandma in the back saying twenty-five miles an hour was quite fast enough. On the outskirts of town we spent an agonising ten minutes creeping along behind a milk float. Grandpa never attempts to overtake, unlike Dad, who is accused by Mum of reckless driving whenever he tries to pass tractors and "Sunday afternoon drivers" as he calls them. In Dad's opinion, Grandpa is the ultimate Sunday afternoon driver.

When the milk float finally rattled into a side road I shouted, "Go, Grandpa, quick!" but it was too late: before he could apply sufficient pressure to the accelerator, a second milk float had pulled out in front of us, as though by design. It was gone half-past nine when we drew up in the yard at Pampered Pup Kennels.

Anyone who has never visited a kennels, and would like to know the general effect, should try to imagine the noise of about fifty dogs, hidden away behind high walls, all barking at once: high barks, low barks, fast barks, slow barks, the yapping of small Dachshunds and the Beware-of-the-Dog bow-wowing of Dalmatians and Dobermans. I suppose it must be like that all the time – it's just as well there are no houses nearby. Of course most of the dogs are only there for a short stay, so perhaps they never really have a chance to calm down and get used to being pampered.

We asked at the desk, and to my great relief the receptionist said Yes, they still had Pip. So we went and sat on a bench on a patch of dusty grass and a friendly girl called Janet, dressed in boys' clothes, brought him out to us on a lead. He seemed to be the only dog there who wasn't barking. He was just small enough for me to pick up – a brown and white barrel with short legs and a smooth coat. He had a marking on his back in the shape of a heart, and his ears and the top of his head were dark

and polished-looking. They reminded me of Miss Winterton's mahogany dining table.

"He looks just like Scamp!" I whispered. "So he does!" replied Grandma, who had seen a lot of my drawings of Scamp.

The whole time we were fussing over the rather fat little dog known as Pip, he gazed into the distance and showed no interest in us at all, but it didn't matter. I immediately fell in love with him as I had expected to. I murmured in his ear that we were his family and we hoped he liked us. Janet was saying something about him not being very good with other dogs, but I didn't really pay much attention – it didn't seem to matter just then.

"He's not much of a one for playing either," added Janet. "He won't run after a ball, how*ever* hard you try."

"Perhaps the weather's been too hot for him to play," said Grandma. "But then it would be a shame if he didn't, after you've waited so long for a dog. Should we try somewhere else, do you think?" I replied firmly that I did want Pip, even if he didn't know how to play. (Secretly I was certain I could train him to, although I didn't say it aloud.)

So it only remained for us to fill in a form and pay a small fee, and Pip was free to leave Pampered Pup Kennels and start his new life.

When we reached the car, Grandpa opened Lucy's door and tipped the seat forward ready to coax him in, but he needed no persuasion. He leapt straight onto the back seat as though he knew all about cars and he knew this one was his. I climbed in next to him and he stood panting, his nose to the window.

Being parked in the sun all that time had heated Lucy's interior to egg-frying temperature, and every time I tried to shift my position, my legs stuck painfully to the seat leather. On the way back through town we stopped at an engraver's to have a disc made, with "Pip" on one side (it looks strange now) and Grandma's telephone number on the other. Near the engraver's was a pet shop, where we bought him a red collar and lead,

some Winalot biscuits and two bowls with "Dog" printed on the side in case he had an aptitude for reading.

All the way home in the car he continued panting and looking out of the window, but made no objection when I put my arms lightly round him.

🕮

The grandfather clock was chiming four. I sat on the strip of bare wooden floor under the living room window next to my dog – *my dog!* – who had just been taken for his first walk. He had been on the end of a long rope, but apart from that it had been a proper walk. I didn't stroke him because it was so warm, even in the house. I just watched him and talked quietly to him, until finally he stopped panting, lay down with his nose on his paws and closed his eyes.

I thought back to my old companion, Scamp. He hadn't gone anywhere: he had just changed his name to Pippy. He'd been a real dog all along.

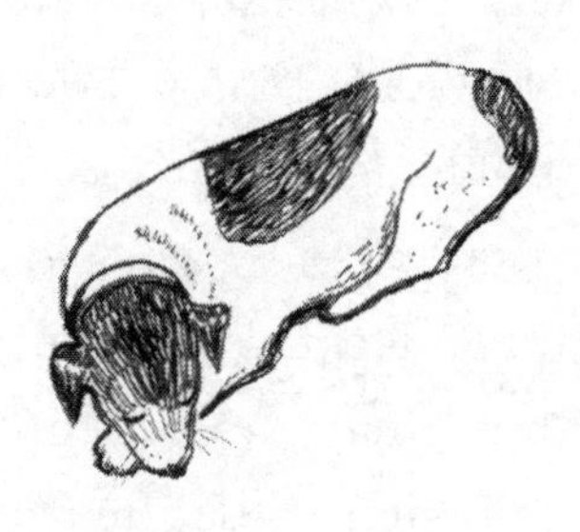

Chapter Five
STAYING UP LATE

Virtues of Pippy the Dog – the train journey – the Midnight Movie – adventures by candlelight – sinister aspect of Grandpa's false teeth – Grandma to the rescue

PIPPY the Dog settled in well at Grandma's house, as anyone would. His aloof manner melted away, and with it his stoutness; his fur became softer, his brown eyes more full of expression. And the dog we grew to know during that first summer was surprisingly well-behaved. He had his faults, there is no doubt, but for now I shall gloss over them and concentrate on his good points.

If we thought he would bring mud into the house, we were wrong. Some dogs will throw themselves heedlessly into a river, or roll with glee in a dreadful-smelling ditch, but Pippy, we have learned, isn't one of that kind. He tiptoes mincingly round the smallest puddle, and he always squeezes along the edge of a muddy path to find the driest route. When he gets home, he spends hours cleaning off whatever dirt has succeeded in attaching itself to him. A fastidious dog.

He yaps when his guard-dog duty requires him to, but he doesn't just stand around yapping for the sake of it, as some dogs do. He doesn't even bark to come into the house, but waits in long-suffering silence on the step until someone lets him in. Sometimes we open the door to go outside and nearly fall over him. A patient dog.

Not satisfied with being cleaner and more demure than anyone could reasonably expect, he further adds to his popularity by getting up late in the mornings. I had braced myself for being woken at dawn by howling or door-scratching, but Pippy seems to enjoy a lie-in as much as I do. Undeniably a civilised dog.

Grandma usually refers to him affectionately as "the pup". Grandpa, I am sorry to say, has always called him just "the dog", which seems off-hand, but I know he loves him as much as we do. I can't imagine life at Grandma's without him now.

At the beginning of the summer holidays this year, it was agreed by Mum and Dad that I was old enough to change trains by myself and travel all the way to Grandma's unaccompanied.

All by myself on such a long journey! Never mind that the trains weren't steam trains; never mind that the windows appeared to have had buckets of mud thrown at them; never mind that as I wheeled my suitcase across the station from the first train to the second, the announcements seemed to be in some language that sounded like English but had no distinguishable English words in it. I found my train by bravely asking a man pushing a trolley, and was glad to discover that it was the kind they always have in films, with closed compartments leading off a corridor. Following Mum's instructions I chose a carriage with two ladies in it, one of whom helped me put my suitcase up on the rack. Then I settled down in a corner in the pleasant knowledge that the hard part of the journey was over.

For a few miles I pretended that I was on my way to a boarding school in the Swiss Alps; then I lay back languidly in my seat with eyes

half-closed and became a famous sleuth keeping my two fellow-travellers under surveillance without their knowledge. I decided that they were probably sisters. One looked cool and composed in a tailored blouse and skirt, and was doing a newspaper crossword. The one who had helped me with my suitcase wore a limp sun-dress, and kept fanning herself with *Woman's Own* and complaining about the heat – to the slight disapproval of the first, I thought. I tried to work out which one was older, and to deduce from their occasional remarks what kind of families they had and why they were travelling.

The ticket inspector slid the carriage door open without warning and made me jump, putting an end to my career as a suave private investigator, so I turned instead to staring out of the dirt-spattered window and composing majestic poetry in my head about golden cornfields encircled by sheltering hills, then gave it up and just blinked rhythmically as the telegraph poles flew by. I did try to read, but it was hard to concentrate and I kept on reading the same sentence.

The train stopped at the last station before mine and my companions got out. They very kindly asked me if I was going to be all right getting off at my station, and helped me pull my suitcase down in readiness. From then on I sat on the edge of the seat holding my case tightly, and concentrating very hard so as not to miss my station and be carried on to the end of the line. As the train began to slacken its speed I moved to the door and began dragging the window down so that I could put my arm out and turn the handle the moment we drew into the station. I felt grey of hand and grey of face after the journey, and for once was quite looking forward to washing.

Grandpa was standing on the platform in the shade of the wooden canopy, dressed in his linen suit and panama hat, and looking anxiously up and down the train for me. When he saw me his face cleared, then his jaw dropped in exaggerated amazement.

"Good heavens, you've grown about a foot since Easter!" And in his hooting Miss Perkins voice he added, "A-*pooh,* child! We must put a *brrrick* on your head!"

We both laughed nervously, and he took my case and led the way to a telephone box, so that I could ring Mum and let her know I had arrived safely.

Lucy was waiting for us in the station car park. As I climbed into the passenger seat Grandpa dropped a shiny fifty-new-pence piece into my hand, and then looked as if he didn't know anything about it. I smiled, but couldn't think of anything to say. I wished Mum had been there to do the talking, even though it would have meant me being squashed in the back with the bags while she went on about Harold Wilson or Edward Heath or both.

After a longish silence we began a rather stilted conversation about school, and then moved onto my week at the seaside with Mum and Dad, and every so often I had to tell Grandpa which gear he should be in, because he didn't always notice when he was in the wrong one. I do know something about gears, because when I was small Dad used to let me sit on his knee and steer our Hillman Minx round the disused airfield near our house, while he operated the pedals and explained how the clutch worked.

We turned off the main road and chugged into the village from the bottom end, all our conversation used up for the time being. I gave silent greetings to Water Lane, the allotments, the church and the shops, and to Sam's farm, which is on the corner where Grandma's lane runs into the village street. Ned, the farm collie, came up to the open gate and barked at us half-heartedly. Just past the farm we had to squeeze Lucy into the bank to let Sam get by in his tractor; he grinned, holding his thumbs up with his hands still on the wheel, and disappeared from sight as he passed us very close, level with Lucy's roof. Sam has curly yellow hair, a bit thin on top, and a weather-tanned face. I always feel he is laughing at me just a little, I'm not sure why.

The lane continued to slope gently upwards, and began making its long curve past Grandma's orchard and garden. There was Grandma's hedge; there were the steps in the bank leading up to the orchard gate;

there was the thatched roof, the white wall, the end room chimney and the telephone wire strung across the lane. There it all was, waiting.

The gate stood open to welcome us. Grandpa drove slowly into the yard and Lucy stopped with a jerk. There was a moment of profound silence. Then Pippy began barking from inside the house, and we climbed out of the car.

Grandma emerged from the open kitchen door in her apron, behind Pippy, who had already jumped into my arms. I tried to kiss him and Grandma at the same time, but it was difficult to manage either with him wriggling and licking my face, and repeatedly throwing his head up and hitting me on the chin. Eventually I had to put him down and let him run round the yard a few times to work off his excitement. Grandpa reached into the back of the car for my suitcase, and suddenly I didn't feel shy any more.

"Thank you, Lurch," I said, and Lurch simpered and touched his hat. I stretched myself and turned slowly round and round with my arms above my head, gazing up at Grandma's sky.

🕮

We usually have a hot mid-day dinner at Grandma's, even in warm weather. The day I arrived it was roast chicken, always kept for special occasions, followed by gooseberry pie and custard.

"No washing up on your first day," said Grandma afterwards. "You just go and please yourself, and we'll go out for a walk later on. Oh, wait – what do you think of this idea?"

Glancing furtively over her shoulder at Grandpa, who was humming something classical at the sink, she fished out the *Radio Times* from a pile of garden catalogues and money-off coupons and handed it to me, pointing to the item at the end of that day's listings.

"10.40 Midnight Movie, *The Curse of Owl Manor*," it said, followed by "12.05 Closedown."

"The odd late night doesn't really matter so much now you're older," whispered Grandma, seeing my look of surprise. "And if it gets too frightening we can always…"

But she had to mime with her hand the act of turning the volume down, the end of the sentence having been engulfed in one of her silent laughter attacks, which I couldn't help joining in with, despite having no idea what had prompted it. We both tottered into the living room, where Grandma leaned on the settle for support and I fell backwards into Grandpa's armchair. Pippy, who had been patiently waiting in his bed for some more attention, galloped across the hearthrug and leapt into the air, landing on my lap with his usual precision at the same moment as I hit the chair.

🕮

Dusk had fallen, and Grandma had lit a small fire in honour of the occasion. The clock struck ten out in the hall. Forty minutes still to go! I had been sitting at the table in my pyjamas and dressing gown since nine o'clock, whiling away the time by writing yet another story, no doubt doomed to be unfinished like all the others, in yet another Silvine exercise book. I was writing it with a magnificently fat biro, new in at the Post Office Stores. It had four points, red, blue, green and black, which you selected by sliding different buttons up and down. I yawned as discreetly as I could and re-read my first page.

THE HAUNTED TOWER, CHAPTER ONE. Miranda stared through the mullioned window at the incessant rain, and sighed.

The name "Miranda" had a large red-and-blue initial M decorated with green leaves and tendrils, like the illuminated letters you see in old manuscripts. I thought "mullioned" sounded romantic, and made a mental note to look it up in the dictionary another day.

She heard a creaking sound, as if someone somewhere was opening a door very slowly. But there was no-one else in the house… Miranda started from the window seat and ventured into the great hall to investigate.

I had done my best to make the writing look like printing, with hooks on the letters, and well-rounded commas and full stops. The three dots after the word "house", indicating mystery and suspense, had grown out of all proportion to the other punctuation as I had worked over and over them trying to make them perfectly circular.

The rest of the page was devoted to a thickly-shaded drawing (done with the black biro point) of a girl with ringlets and a long trailing skirt, carrying a candle raised high with a halo of light round it. Her arm didn't look quite right, but the overall effect was good.

My eyes fell shut, and I blinked them open again. I fiddled with the buttons on my biro and waited for inspiration, but could form no idea of what Miranda would do next. Grandpa, who had dozed off in his chair while reading *The Daughter of Time*, woke up and announced that he was off to bed. "Don't stay up too late," he added, still affecting to know nothing of our plans for the evening.

Grandma rolled up her knitting. "How about a cup of tea to help you keep awake? Anything to eat? It's a long time since tea. I think I fancy a bit of bread-and-dripping. "

By the time we had drunk our cups of tea, and I had eaten two Jaffa Cakes leaving the middles until last, and Grandma had taken advantage of Grandpa's absence to give the end of her bread-and-dripping to an attentive Pippy, it was finally time to tune in. Grandma opened the doors to the television cabinet with a flourish and turned the knob. No sooner had the greyish picture flickered on, than thick black horizontal bands began to roll brokenly up the screen; but Grandma gave the side of the cabinet a practised thump to stabilise the vertical hold and settled down in her armchair.

The Curse of Owl Manor was well worth waiting for. It was an old film, featuring a decrepit and gloomy house with a supposedly empty east wing from which blood-curdling cries were heard in the night. There were also lighted candles in rooms that were supposed to be uninhabited, windows that burst open for no reason and let the curtains flap wildly, a menacing butler with a silver tray and shifty eyes, and a great deal of very bad weather. The heroine wore a floating white dress and screamed more than she need have done. We kept the volume low so she wouldn't wake Grandpa, who was in bed directly above us, but we weren't frightened enough to turn the sound right off. Pippy took no interest at all and slept peacefully behind Grandma's chair all the way through.

When it was over, transmission came to an end for the evening and the picture turned to a snowstorm, accompanied by a loud hissing noise. I turned off the television and watched the snowstorm shrink to a bright little dot and disappear.

We sat for a while talking about the film and watching the fire go out. I scraped the end of the poker in the ash on the hearth and made clumsy patterns with it. The front of the fire basket reminded me of a portcullis in a medieval castle. Behind it I could see mountains, cliffs and chasms in the dying embers of the fire, and a great many faces – a cow, a dog, an Easter Island statue, a witch with a hooked nose. Light flickered on and off the edges of the strange forms, and every now and then a wisp of hot flame shot up and disappeared again. When I poked the embers they grew brighter – almost unbearably bright. They roasted my face and hand, even though the fire was nearly out. The grey shapes in the ash looked solid, but they disintegrated at the slightest touch of the poker, and the fragments of charred wood that were left tinkled as I raked the ash through into the bottom of the fire.

There was a sudden yawn from behind the armchair. "Gracious!" said Grandma. "The pup hasn't been out since before tea!" Pippy jumped up and headed for the door, and Grandma brushed some crumbs off her skirt onto the hearth. "Why don't you put on your wellingtons," she said to me over her shoulder, "and come out in your dressing gown? A bit of fresh air before you go to bed."

I fetched my boots from the hall and put them on by the kitchen door, while Pippy scrabbled on the lino in his haste to get outside. The night air felt crisp and cool. We walked thirty yards up the lane and back again, talking quietly so as not to disturb roosting birds and other sleeping creatures. Pippy's nails clicked on the surface of the road. As we drew near the gate, his elongated shadow, cast by the lamp on the end of the house, looked like that of a wolf.

Then, in a moment, the shadow was gone and so was he. We were enveloped in

blackness. Not only the outside light but also the one in the kitchen had been extinguished.

"Oh! A power cut!" exclaimed Grandma. "A good thing it waited until the film was over."

It was a strange feeling to be in absolute darkness, without the least glimmer of light anywhere. There were no stars showing, nor the thinnest slice of moon. I felt Pippy against my leg and picked him up so as not to trip over him. Fumbling for the catch on the gate I walked very carefully across the yard to the kitchen door with one hand out in front. Grandma followed, holding on to my dressing-gown cord. I pushed the door open, felt around on the wall for the light switch and tried it – nothing. Grandma groped her way along the cupboards until she reached the odds-and-ends drawer, and chuckled invisibly to herself as she rummaged for candles and matches. "I was just thinking of Grandpa fast asleep through it," she said.

Pippy finished noisily lapping water from his bowl, and we heard the *tink-tink* of his collar as he trotted off into the living room to his bed. Evidently he could see in the dark.

Grandma lit a stub of lumpy white candle, allowed a trickle of wax to drip down and used it to stick the candle to an old cracked saucer. Then she reached into the back of a cupboard for her only proper candle-holder, and fixed a more presentable candle into it to give to me.

"We could make good shadows with these," I suggested. So we put the candles on the table and made bird shadows on the wall with our hands. They weren't neat and tidy like the shadows cast by an electric light. Their wings stretched madly outwards and then shrank back again, as if they were auditioning for a part in a midnight movie.

Grandma made her bird flutter down and land on the back of the chair. "We'd better stop this and get to bed," she said. "We could wait all night for the lights to come back on."

We crept through the living room and into the hall, holding high our candles. We took turns to visit the Lav, shivering, and by arrangement pulled the chain only once. The noise it made, exploding on the stillness

of the night, seemed enough to wake sleepers for miles around, and we hurried into the middle room to escape it. I led the way up the stairs, making good use of the rope-handrail, and our shadows dipped and swooped across the curving wall.

"Spooks!" said Grandma in a sepulchral voice, and then "Glory be!" followed by more stifled laughter, as she grabbed first the rope's shadow and then the rope itself to stop herself falling.

Although I had often imagined a shuttered east wing in Grandma's house where ashen-faced prisoners languished awaiting rescue, I was glad at that moment that no such place existed. Even by candlelight the house felt benign, as though all who had lived in it through the long centuries had been content. There were no ghosts here.

It was only when I was standing on the top stair, next to the bathroom door, that I remembered Grandpa's false teeth, grinning in their blue plastic mug on the back of the wash-basin.

Of course false teeth are quite an ordinary thing, and plenty of people have them. Grandma doesn't – she has her own interesting teeth with gold bits here and there – but Grandpa's are white and even, and live in the tooth-mug when he isn't wearing them. When I was small I was afraid of them and wouldn't go into the bathroom if they were there. Now I'm older I don't usually mind them – but false teeth by candlelight!

"Grandma!"

"Yes, my lady?" said Grandma. Inspired by the film, she assumed the role of butler in Grandpa's absence.

"Could you take Grandpa's teeth out of the bathroom while I go in there?"

Grandma obligingly went in to get them, and I hid in my bedroom across the landing until I heard her whisper, in her own voice, "It's all right, they've gone." And then, "Everything is in readiness, my lady. Will there be anything else tonight, my lady?"

"No thank you, Glyde, that will be all," I replied bravely.

I knew that I could trust Grandma not to play any tricks on me with the teeth – practical jokes are not her cup of tea at all. She's not the sort

of person who would ever tie your shoe laces together or put a rubber snake in your bed. Mum just might have been tempted to creep back with the teeth when I was in the bathroom and make them gnash at me round the half-open door, but Grandma would not dream of doing such a thing. Nevertheless, the flickering candlelight gave me the edgy feeling that the teeth might somehow come back by themselves, and I was in my bedroom in less than a minute. I blew out the candle, jumped straight into the cool bed and lay there with the sheet pulled up under my chin and my eyes staring into nothing, watching for "spooks". Usually the light from the landing slides in under my door at night, and I can make out the shapes of the pictures on the wall and my dressing-gown on the back of the door – but not tonight. The dark lay on my face like a black blanket. How odd, to have my eyes wide open and yet see nothing!

I pulled the sheet up over my nose. The only sound I could hear was Grandpa snoring, a peculiar rising and falling noise which sounds like someone playing the lowest notes on the piano. Once when I was quite young I was woken in the night by it and went downstairs to see if someone *was* playing the piano. Grandma thought that showed great pluck.

After a few minutes the snoring subsided, and I heard Grandma go into the bathroom and start running water – a much more reassuring sound. In a few moments she would come in with her candle, to say prayers and kiss me goodnight.

The next thing I knew, she was standing by the bed with my morning tea, much later than usual, and sunlight filled the room.

Chapter Six
SPRING CLEANING

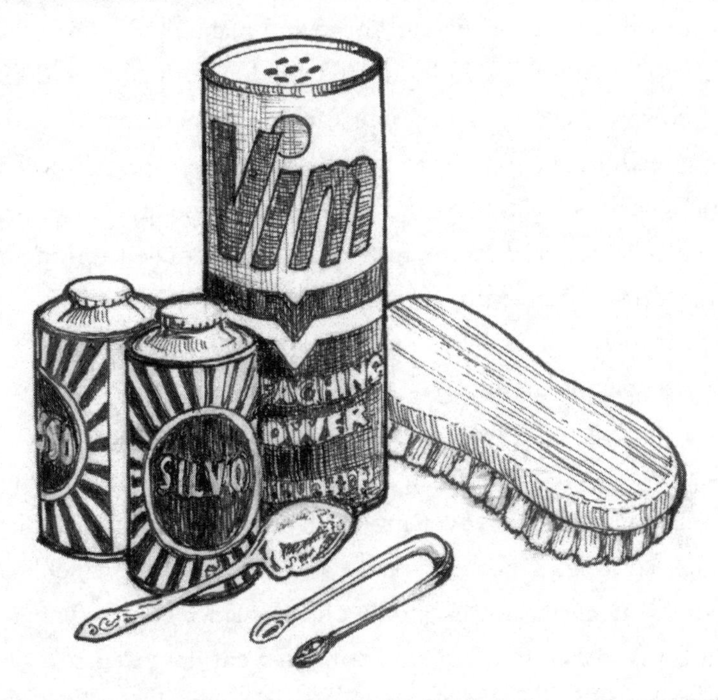

Cobwebs and mild disorder in the home – rewards of teamwork – a dog's natural suspicions of spring cleaning shown to be justified – a job well done

I DO try hard not to be bossy, but sometimes it gets out. One afternoon, after spending an hour hunting unsuccessfully for the chess board and finding quantities of cobwebs which had long ceased to be of interest to the spiders, I informed Grandma that her house needed spring cleaning.

"Does it?" said Grandma. "Well, now you mention it, I suppose it's a few years since it was last done properly. We'll do it after you've gone home, and call it autumn cleaning."

"Why don't we do it now? I could help. The weather's not too hot. Spring cleaning is fun, you know, Grandma."

"Fun?" squeaked Grandma in disbelief. "Spending three days of your holiday doing chores?"

"Why not? I've helped spring clean at home – it's like an adventure. The house looks all strange and different and you find loads of things you've lost."

"Well, Grandpa would certainly enjoy it. He's the tidiest person I know." Grandma looked at me doubtfully. "All right then, if you're sure you want to. But we needn't carry on if you get fed up."

That was as good as a challenge. I decided on the spot that even if I did get fed up, I wasn't going to admit it to anyone.

Grandpa agreed that spring cleaning was long overdue, and Grandpa is a man of action. The very next day, out came the Brasso and the Vim, the mop and the scrubbing brush, the carpet beater and the feather duster, and by mid-morning the dining chairs were upside down on the table, mattresses stood propped up in the garden getting air round them, cupboards and bookcases stood away from the walls, and all the silver – teapot, sugar bowl, spoons, sugar tongs and the rest – which reposed in the grandeur of the sideboard most of the year and seemed like treasures from a far-off land, waited humbly on the kitchen table with the coal scuttle and fire irons, ready for polishing to a fine shine. During the course of the first day all the blankets were shaken outside. The curtains were taken down and some were washed; others just had the dust shaken out of them.

Grandpa is ideally suited to spring cleaning, because once he has begun a task, he doesn't leave it until it is done to perfection. He persevered happily for hours at jobs Grandma would have been impatient with, such as scrubbing the stove so thoroughly inside and out with a brillo pad that it seemed a shame to spoil it by cooking anything.

People spring cleaning deserve plenty of breaks. Every couple of hours we would take ourselves outside for tea and biscuits or a picnic lunch in the garden, letting the breeze blow the dust out of our hair. When we'd had enough of a rest we would go round the house inspecting each other's handiwork before we started again. Having your work admired by someone else inspires you to keep going, if by chance you have secretly begun to feel a little weary of the whole business. And, of

course, it's always encouraging to know that everyone else is working as hard as you are.

Spring cleaning really *is* a sort of adventure, if you look at it the right way. During one of our breaks, the mirror from above the end room fireplace was leaning on the well, its back laced with cobwebs. I turned it round and studied the garden in reflection – an unfamiliar paradise lived in by people we didn't know. On a crazy-paved path in the mirrored world stood fourteen pairs of boots and shoes, lined up in neat rows for polishing, as if waiting for a dance to begin.

Cleaning Grandma's living room carpet was hard work. The vacuum cleaner couldn't suck up all Pippy's short white hairs – they had woven themselves in too well. No doubt the brown ones had too, but they didn't show. The only way to remove the hairs was to brush them with the carpet brush, which has thick, stiff bristles like the twigs of a tree. Now I come to think of it, I suppose they *are* the twigs of a tree. Dust puffed up into my face, and the brush made an unpleasant rasping noise, but the carpet looked so much better that it was worth the effort. Afterwards the bare floorboards round the edge of the room had to be swept with a soft brush and polished on hands and knees.

I should really have shampooed the carpet next, but at that moment the job held no appeal, so I put the dining chairs back on the floor the right way up, sat down on one and began polishing the table. This was a lazy thing to do, because the table is regularly polished anyway, but it was pleasing to sit there dreamily pushing the duster, an old vest of Grandma's, slowly back and forth across the smooth surface, while Grandpa vacuumed in the middle room. As I polished I hummed a strange droning tune to myself – a duet for voice and vacuum cleaner.

Grandma, meanwhile, was washing the bed linen – an arduous job requiring her to lift the heavy wet sheets out of the washing machine with a pair of wooden tongs and feed them into the mangle. The two rollers squeeze out the water, and the clothes come out the other side as stiff as boards. Mum threw out her mangle years ago and got a spin-drier, but Grandma doesn't throw anything out as long as it works.

A steamy sort of dishcloth smell always fills the kitchen while the washing is being done. If Grandma ever has to wash in wet weather she lets down the airer from the ceiling and hangs the clothes on that, or drapes them round the fire on a clothes-horse, but today, with the sky blue and the clouds high, she pegged everything out on the line in the garden and then hoisted it up with the prop. The sheets and bedcovers billowed joyfully in the breeze.

The next day, we hung all the small rugs and door-mats out on the clothes-line and took turns beating them with the carpet beater. Grandma let out cries of gratified horror when she saw the air all around her grey with dust. She was really quite enjoying herself, now that we were halfway through and she was beginning to see good results. The beating was hot work, though, and I was glad that my next task was to be cleaning the larder.

The larder is the coolest room in a cool house: its tiny window receives hardly any sun. Grandma has never had to bother with a fridge. She keeps her milk bottles in a pail of cold water on the larder floor, and if we want ice cream we buy a block of Cornish at the Post Office Stores, bring it home wrapped in newspaper to slow down its melting and eat it straight away.

Across one end of the larder is a low, tiled shelf with the meat-safe underneath it. The meat-safe is a green metal cupboard with holes in it which are large enough to let air circulate around the meat but too small to let flies in. Higher up around the larder walls run several narrow shelves on which stand pots of home-made raspberry, plum and blackcurrant jam, and a row of hefty jars of brown pickled onions, much stronger-flavoured than the little white ones you buy in the shops. There are also bottles of ketchup, vinegar and salad cream, and a gravy browning bottle which always drips down itself and sticks to the shelf. I stood on a chair to wipe and re-arrange all these bottles, along with about forty

cans of various kinds of fruit, baked beans, spaghetti hoops and spam. Mum has always said Grandma and Grandpa could withstand a long siege. When we first learned about besieged towns in history at school, I visualised Grandma's larder, with turrets.

The spam tins, squarish in shape, are greatly superior to the normal kind of can. To open a can of fruit or baked beans you have to stab the point of a tin-opener into the lid, trying to land it as close as possible to the edge of the tin without missing the tin completely, then grind your way all the way round, creating a horrible jagged edge which the food catches on when you pour it out. But to open a spam tin you just break off the special key from the lid, fit it onto a tab at the side and wind it round until the lid lifts up like the lid of a trunk, leaving the key dangling at the side with a long strip of metal coiled round it. Grandma always lets me be the one to open the spam.

Having wiped all the tins, I turned my attention to the low, white-tiled shelf on which stood a collection of old crazed bowls, covered with chipped saucers. These bowls contained all manner of interesting left-overs – two cold sausages, a few tinned peaches, a slice of custard tart. I decided to tidy away the leftovers by eating them – with the exception of some whiskered prunes from the very back of the shelf, which I carried at arm's length to the compost heap.

The only member of the household who didn't seem to be enjoying the spring cleaning was Pippy the Unadventurous Dog. He hated the noise of the vacuum cleaner, and would skulk away from it into corners or even go outside in disgust. He didn't like everything being out of place, and it had not escaped his notice that we were too busy to give him his usual daily walk. He took a particularly dim view of his bed being dismantled and washed on the morning of the third day, and refused to let me throw away all the old bone fragments I found in it. Each time I tried to pick one up he gave a polite little snarl to indicate that he would be forced to take some kind of action if I persisted. In the end I shook the pieces of bone out into a pile on the lawn and left him guarding

them, lying with his nose on his paws and watching me distrustfully as I went back into the house.

The last straw for Pippy was my decision halfway through that morning to give him a bath. I knew his opinion of baths and sympathised, but surely there could be no place for a grubby dog in so clean a house, and it did seem wise to get it over with before Grandpa started cleaning the bathroom.

When I first called him he jumped up and reported eagerly for duty – perhaps he thought he was about to be taken for a decent walk at last, poor thing. But seeing me at the bottom of the stairs with my sleeves rolled up and a washing-up bowl in my hand, he realised with a suddenly sinking heart what was in store for him and retreated rapidly. Usually he creeps into his bed and pretends not to exist when a bath is proposed, but his bed wasn't there in its place under the settle, so he cowered on the hearthrug instead, waiting for the inevitable.

"It's all right, little Pip, it won't take long," I said soothingly as I picked him up. He made no resistance whatever to being carried upstairs, just hung in limp resignation from my arm. I closed the bathroom door to be sure he didn't try to leave, and placed the washing-up bowl in the bottom of the bath while he looked despairingly on. I ran warm water into the bowl and added a drop of washing-up liquid for that luxury bubble-bath effect. Then I took off his collar – the final confirmation of doom.

He submitted in speechless sorrow to being set down in the bowl, scrubbed from ears to tail and ignominiously rinsed with Grandma's pink shower hose. He wasn't the only one suffering: the rinsing was difficult, because the shower hose has round ends and Grandma's taps are square; this meant that the hose-ends kept popping off the taps and having to be forced back on. I also had to be quick to turn off one tap whenever the hose slipped off the other one, in order to stop very hot or cold water rushing down the pipe.

Once the rinsing was finished the wretched, drooping creature in the washing-up bowl seemed to regain a little of his normal spirit. He shook

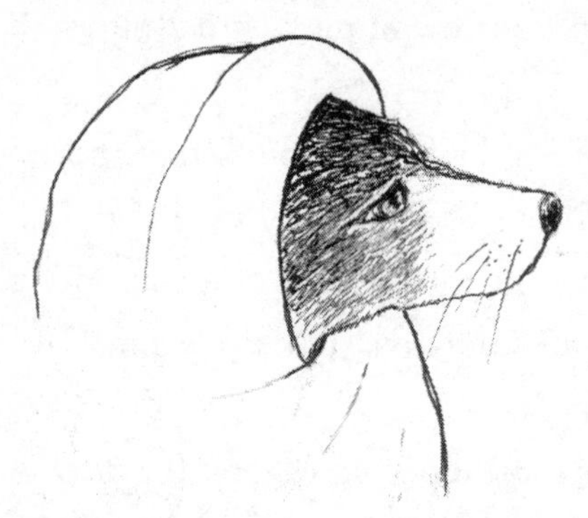

himself and made me nearly as wet as he was, then struggled as I lifted him out onto the bath mat and wrapped him in a towel to rub him down. In no time he began to cheer up and look on the bright side of life. He isn't one to bear a grudge and, after all, he would soon be so delightfully sweet-smelling and fluffy that he would probably be in great demand as a lap-dog that evening. Perhaps it was almost worth all the misery. I put his collar back on and opened the door, and he scampered downstairs into the garden to lick himself dry.

My last spring cleaning task was to sort out the odds-and-ends drawer in the kitchen. Grandma was rather worried about this, because the odds-and-ends drawer is the sort of place where you look for a screw, a rubber band, a paper bag or a missing piece of something, and you are almost guaranteed to find what you are looking for if you rummage long enough. Grandma felt certain that if anything in the drawer was thrown away, we should want that very item the following week. She only let me clear it out when I promised to collect all the rubbish in a bag, label it and put it on a shelf in the outhouse, just in case. There was no room in the dustbin anyway: never normally more than half full, it now had its lid perched high and looked like one of those overflowing "trash cans" in *Top Cat*.

I had just finished the drawer and wiped the kitchen table when Grandma came in to make a sponge cake for tea. I sat at the other end of the table to stick all the loose Green Shield stamps I had found in the drawer into Grandma's Saver Books. I like licking the stamps – the glue on them is the tasty kind, and it is always satisfying to tidy them away into books. Normally Grandma uses her stamps to get trifling things like packets of paper doilies, bath salts or gadgets for opening bottles. The grandest thing she has ever sent off for is an instant camera, which she brings out for my visits and in between forgets how to use. But this time the stamps had been allowed to build up into an impressive collection.

The books rapidly filled up and the pages became stiff, like the parchment pages of ancient documents.

"You've got enough stamps here for an electric blanket, Grandma! Or a hairdryer and some curling tongs. Or you could keep on collecting and get one of those big food mixers."

"Oh dear me!" said Grandma. "Let's ask your mother when she comes. Perhaps she'd like something."

I finished my sticking and scraped out Grandma's mixing bowl. Sponge cake mixture is so much better before it's cooked that I often wonder why it isn't served as a pudding just as it is.

While the cake cooked in an *Ideal Home* sort of way in the sparklingly clean oven, I settled down to write two postcards which I had found in the bottom of the drawer. They both had the same picture of a row of thatched cottages under an unlikely turquoise sky, and one had a sticky brown mark on it. I decided to tidy them away by sending the sticky one to Mum and Dad, and the other to my best friend Alison. Alison would probably be home from her holidays by now. She had gone to a place called Ibeetha, which Dad had told me to my surprise was spelt I-b-i-z-a.

"Hope you had a nice time in Ibiza," I wrote casually in my loopiest handwriting.

📖

I don't think I can really describe the satisfaction of sitting down at the end of those three days knowing that the whole house was as tidy as it could possibly be, glowing with cleanliness and subtly scented with "Thousand-and-one". All the beds were freshly made, clothes lay neatly folded on wardrobe shelves, books and bookshelves were free of dust, no sweet papers lurked under armchair cushions, the bath was spotless except for the drippy green marks below the taps that still would *not* come off, in spite of Grandpa's patient applications of lemon juice; no sooty webs hung about the chimney-place, and even the light bulbs had been washed. The bacon cupboard and the corn cupboard had been emptied, dusted out and re-filled, and I had helped Grandma sort her needlework remnants, throwing out a few useless bits of cloth into the compost and

putting the rest back in the drawers, rolled into neat bundles with the frayed ends trimmed off. Finally, Grandpa had tidied out the drawers of his bureau and had found the chess board in the bottom of one of them.

Feeling thoroughly and justifiably pleased with ourselves, we three workers stretched out our legs in the end room armchairs, benignly full of bread-and-butter, cold ham and freshly-made sponge cake eaten off the best china. With sighs of complacency we admired the vase of garden flowers in the fireplace and the chess men set out on the board, each piece in the mathematical centre of its square.

Pippy the Fragrant Dog, having enjoyed his own helping of ham, lay contentedly on my knee. The bath and other indignities were all forgiven. He wouldn't be allowed to wipe his chops on the carpet for a while, but that would soon pass, and everything would be back to normal.

Chapter Seven
A RED-LETTER DAY

Afternoons out – Grandma puts her face on – Old Tom and the village shops – fishing in the stream – an unlooked-for reward – the fish go free

MORNINGS at Grandma's are for household chores, gardening, messing about or paw-cleaning, depending on who you are. But afternoons are for Going Out.

We may go for a long walk to the knoll, or a short one to the stream, or take a turn down Vicarage Lane to look at the new houses and come home through the churchyard. I can never resist trying the handle of the tiny, cobwebbed door at the back of the church, but it's always locked. Now and again for a treat we catch the bus to town and go to the shops and the park. Quite often we used to walk to the railway embankment and watch for the occasional train, but now that the branch line has closed, to Grandpa's great annoyance, we won't even see a goods train trundling along it any more.

When I was younger, Grandma and I used to go to the wood on the far side of Sam's fields and pretend to make cowboy films. It was a good game, inspired by a television programme I had seen about film directors. Grandma's job was to roll an imaginary camera and call out "Take One!" "Action!" and "Cut!" while I galloped about jumping logs, hiding behind trees and rolling down slopes to dodge bullets or arrows. Often too, in those days, we would go down to the farm to look at the cows and the chickens and talk to Ned the collie – but that was before we had a Jack Russell terrier joining us on our outings.

Grandpa doesn't usually come on these excursions, preferring to play the piano or potter in his greenhouse, but from time to time he gets Lucy out and takes us all to the hills for the afternoon. The road runs gently up through acres of sun-dappled forest onto open, brackeny tops where I hunt for whortleberries among the heather and Grandma and Grandpa sit on a log seat facing the distant sea.

🕮

We had finished the spring cleaning just in time. The following day was far too hot for anything so energetic.

"What are we going to do this afternoon?" asked Grandma. "It ought to be something cool and shady, I should think." She had changed into her lightest summer frock, and was seated at her dressing table putting her face on – dabbing powder onto her nose and cheeks with a pink powder puff and making strange shapes with her mouth as ladies must when they have just applied their lipstick.

Fishing was the coolest and shadiest activity I could think of – but with a net, and strictly for minnows only.

Three o'clock found us ambling slowly down through the village to the stream, lazy in the heat. Pippy wasn't even bothering to pull on his lead. I carried my net and jar, Grandma a folding stool and a bag containing her knitting. The large pickle-jar, with a string handle tied very tightly round its neck by Grandpa years before, was a veteran of many fishing expeditions.

We passed several cottages, some thatched, some tiled, and then my favourite village house, a long, low one the colour of strawberry ice cream with "Denhams" carved on the gate and hollyhocks reaching to the upstairs windows. Two sisters, the Misses Crane, live at Denhams. Grandma knows them slightly: they are both retired schoolmistresses. They have a seventy-year-old parrot called The Captain, who in his youth lived "below stairs" in a big house, and to this day is occasionally heard through an open window giving orders to ghostly kitchen maids.

Opposite Denhams, on top of a high bank, stands the old village school, where Miss Agnes Crane used to be headmistress. The school closed a few years ago and was made into a house. The steep, terraced garden in front of it is inhabited by a colony of bright red and blue garden gnomes, some sitting on rocks, some fishing in miniature pools, one even lying in a hammock. I don't know what opinion the Misses Crane have of the gnomes, but Grandpa regards them as an eyesore, and thinks they ought to require planning permission. Grandma and I are not ashamed of liking the gnomes: we always enjoy counting them and noticing if any have moved, or if a new one has joined them. That afternoon the gnome tally was unchanged at fifteen.

A little further down the road we came to the Post Office Stores and the butcher's shop. There was Old Tom sitting in his place on the bench outside, smoking his pipe and dressed, as always, in a crumpled black suit with a waistcoat and a flat cap. He asked us what day it was and we told him. Grandma had a little chat with him and waved to Mr Ackland the butcher through the hanging chains in the doorway.

Mr Robert Ackland is quite young, I think. He has frizzy hair and very red cheeks and wears a striped apron. His shop is always cool, behind its low green awning; it has tiled walls and a tiled floor, with a meat counter on one side and a fish counter on the other, and there are things hanging up in the back which you don't want to look too closely at. Mr Ackland's

hands are as red as his cheeks, and his fingers really do look exactly like sausages. He is jovial and friendly, which is just as well as he has quite a fearsome-looking hatchet in his hand much of the time. When he saw us he came to the door without his hatchet, pushed aside the chains and eyed my fishing net.

"Having fish for supper? Don't catch too many now, or you'll be putting me out of business."

Grandma told me to wait with Pippy while she popped into the Stores for a pot of fish food. Old Tom's pipe had gone out. I sat down on the shop doorstep, wedged Pippy firmly between my knees and watched the re-lighting ceremony.

Shaking out some tobacco from a small flat tin into one cupped hand, Tom leaned forward with the pipe in his other hand and his elbow on his knee. Carefully he tipped the brown shreds of tobacco into the bowl of the pipe and pressed them down with his thumb; then, sliding the pipe between his teeth, he lit a match, put it to the pipe and alternately sucked the stalk of the pipe and puffed smoke out of the corner of his mouth as it got going. The spent match he threw down onto the pavement, where it continued to give off smoke for quite some time. Mrs Studley would have that to sweep up later, I supposed.

The pipe smelt good in the open air. Tom slowly took out his heavy silver pocket-watch and looked at the time, then squinted up at the sun to verify what the watch had told him before replacing it in his waistcoat pocket. Finally he crossed his feet and settled back contentedly on the bench to puff and watch life go by.

It was hot in the shop doorway, and Pippy was straining to be off. Grandma had meant to be in and out of the Stores in two minutes, but Mrs Studley was at her most talkative. I could tell that Grandma was trying to bring the conversation to a close, so I stood up and stepped into the shop, leaving Pippy just outside on the end of his lead. But still Mrs Studley didn't take the hint, and began asking after Grandpa. Grandma replied that he had fulfilled all his spring cleaning duties to perfection and was now planning to tidy out his sheds – as if they needed tidying.

"Well, my love," said Mrs Studley, "he's a treasure – make the most of him. They're not all like that, are they? My Jim now, he's a dreadful untidy man in a shed. In the house now, he's not so bad, but then he's got me watching him." At this point she threw me a big wink, which gave Grandma her opportunity. She looked round as though she had forgotten I was there.

"Goodness, you are patient," she said, and began moving sideways towards the door. "It's terribly hot. We must get to the stream and some shade for Pippy. Good-bye, Mrs Studley."

"Good-bye, my loves. We girls do like a bit of a chat sometimes, don't we?"

I stepped back outside, and Pippy pulled across to sniff Old Tom's shoe. "There now, good boy," said Old Tom, leaning down and tickling Pippy's ears.

We said good-bye to Tom and set off along the side of the churchyard wall, past a pair of cottages with doors opening straight onto the street, past the end of Vicarage Lane, the village hall and the Manor House railings, and round the corner into Water Lane, which runs down between the Manor House garden and one of Sam's fields. We let Pippy off the lead and dawdled along beside the boundary wall of the Manor House under the welcome shade of tall trees. At the end of the lane the stream and the fish were waiting for us.

The stream comes out from the grounds of the Manor House, flows under a small stone bridge and forms a shallow sunlit pool, over which hangs a long, leaning tree – the sort of tree a panther might like to lie on, watching the water and twitching its tail. Other trees surround the place, making it sheltered and secret.

Grandma unfolded her stool and settled down on the bridge. She kept glancing up from her knitting to keep an eye on Pippy in case he should wander off, but he seemed content to stay close by. He tried to drink from the stream without getting his feet wet, then lay down further up the bank and dozed off in the shade.

After I had dipped the pickle jar to fill it, I stood it in a level place on the bank and arranged a few small rocks in the bottom so that the fish, when I caught them, would have a grotto to explore. Then I waded into the stream, being careful not to let it overflow my wellingtons. I stood very still and watched the water, looking past the sparkling surface into the depths. Every so often I spotted a shoal of small dark-coloured fish, and swooping with my net I caught two or three, along with threads of water weed and the bits of stick and straw and leaves that you always find floating down a stream. Every time I had a catch I waded to the edge and turned the net inside out to transfer the minnows into the jar.

Grandma didn't interrupt and say it was time to do something else. She never would unless it was absolutely necessary. When I was small I could play for hours in the house or garden, making dens or climbing trees, and she never came to find out what I was up to or to tell me to be careful, only to let me know when a meal was ready.

Grandma can stay still for a very long time. In the mornings she goes into the garden and puts out bacon rind and bread crusts on the lawn for the birds; she stands on the paving to break the bread so that the crumbs fall onto the stones and are easy for the sparrows to find, and waits there quietly while the birds come and peck around her feet. Every evening she puts out food for the foxes and hedgehogs, and is always on the lookout for badgers. I saw one once, when we were out in the lane at dusk: it was just a shape, shambling across the road and gone in a moment.

It would be too crowded in the jar if I put any more fish in, so the next few catches went straight back into the stream. Then I put down my net and stood silently in the water, I don't know how long, dreaming of being a water-nymph.

When we finally did decide it was time to go home, I had to walk very slowly to avoid slopping water out of the jar of fish. Pippy made many trips up and down Water Lane in the time it took us to get to the far end. From that point on, Grandma had to manage him on his lead as well as her other paraphernalia.

The kitchen was delightfully cool after our rather toilsome walk up through the village. Grandma put the kettle on while I stood my jar on the window sill and sprinkled fish food onto the surface of the water. It smelt rather stale, but then fish food always does. It slowly sank and the fish rose to meet it. I watched them darting among the wisps of weed and bouncing their noses off the stones at the bottom of their strange new world.

When Grandma and I came outside with the tea, Grandpa was already sitting waiting on the bench by the greenhouse in his gardening clothes. He had a large white handkerchief on his head, knotted at the corners, to keep the sun off. As I sat down I noticed something under the bench covered with a tea towel, but I didn't ask what it was.

The greenhouse door stood open, wafting sun-baked tomatoes and the bitter, powdery smell of geranium leaves. A very faint engine noise started far up the lane and grew slowly louder: a van went past the gate, along the side of the garden, round the bend in the lane and along the bottom of the orchard, dying away again into silence.

Grandpa finished his tea, cleared his throat and made the following startling announcement.

"You may think I went to the garden this morning, but I didn't. I went on a secret mission." He reached down under the bench. "Close your eyes."

I closed them, and felt something very heavy being placed on my knees.

"This is a present for you," said Grandma's voice, "for all your help with the spring cleaning."

"They only had grey or blue, so I got blue," said Grandpa. "You can open your eyes now."

I opened them. On my lap lay a typewriter. Grandpa had left its lid off so I would see straight away what it was.

"There," said Grandma. "Now you can really get going."

A typewriter is a fine thing, a grown-up and professional thing. It's smooth and shiny, with lots of moving parts. It smells of oil and ink.

A page that you have typed yourself is a fine thing, too. All those beautiful hooked letters and plump commas, almost like real printing. A typewriter inspires you to grand ideas, grander than you might think of writing in a Silvine exercise book.

Using a typewriter is quite hard work, because the keys are stiff and you have to hit them with some force to make a dark enough mark on the paper. When you are getting near the end of a line a warning bell rings, and you then finish the word you are on, or hyphenate it if it's too long, take a brisk hold of the silver lever and pull it across with a stylish flick of the wrist. This slides the carriage back with a pleasing thump, ready for the next line of typing, but you do have to be careful not to knock over your cup of tea. And of course you have to keep stopping to stroke Pippy the Dog, who regards typing as an unwholesome pursuit, not much better than running a bath.

Occasionally, even if you are very careful, your finger misses its aim and gets trapped between two of the keys. By the time you have pulled it out, two or three of the metal stamps that make the letters have jammed together in mid-air on the end of their stalks as if magnetised, and untangling them covers your fingers in ink. So you go and wash your hands to get the worst off, and then you start again. Of course you would get on much more quickly if you knew the right fingers to use, but even so, when you get a rhythm going you can type at quite a rate, and enjoy that *clacka-clacka* noise that real typists make.

Some typewriters have a split ribbon which allows you to type in red. This one didn't, but if it had it would have been *literally* a red-letter day.

For the next two days I typed page after page: at the dining table, in the end room window seat, in an armchair by the fire, in the garden at a folding table set up for me by Grandpa. My perseverance surprised even me. No wonder Miss Blezard, my headmistress when I was at junior school, had told my parents I was "a strange child". (They were not too concerned, having always found Miss Blezard herself rather strange.)

We still went out in the afternoons, because Pippy must have his walk and I must not get a pasty face, but the mornings and evenings were dedicated to my work. The typewriter had given me a new idea – not so much a story as a project – and I was determined that this time it was going to be finished. The longer I typed, the cloudier grew the water in the pickle jar on the kitchen window sill, and the more sluggish became the fish in their small enclosed world, until on the third day Grandma said,

"Those fish are getting bored. Time to take them home."

So that afternoon's walk took us to the stream once more. As I poured the minnows back into their pool they came to life and darted hither and thither, invigorated by the fresh water and rejoicing to be unconfined. Then they regrouped into a shoal and shot out of sight.

The fish were happy, but not as happy as I was. Grandma and Grandpa looked on with amazement as the pile of pages on the dining room table grew higher, and told each other more than once that they had made a good purchase.

Chapter Eight
IDEAS ABOVE HIS STATION

Shortcomings of Pippy and hazards of dog ownership – a further attempt to gain the Upper Paw – we go to town – the shocking case of the After Eight Mints

WE often wonder how Pippy went astray, and why his previous owner never claimed him from the kennels. I once thought up the romantic idea that he might have run away from a circus, but Grandpa replied that he was more likely to have been thrown out of one, and on reflection I had to agree. Training him to jump through hoops was out of the question: he wasn't even interested in the ordinary tricks any self-respecting dog can do. When I threw him a ball he just gave an embarrassed yawn while I went to pick it up myself. When I tossed a stick across the garden, calling "Fetch, Pippy, fetch!" he rolled over to be tickled. Grandma and I stood on the lawn excitedly throwing a beanbag to each other in the hope that he would leap between us and intercept it, but he remained firmly on the ground and looked the other way.

The day after we got him we went to the Post Office Stores to buy a dog licence, and I suddenly saw with new eyes a greyish plastic Bugs Bunny which had been sitting on a shelf near the door for about three years. I was sure it was about to meet its destiny as a toy for Pippy. But after chewing it for a frantic squeaking minute he punctured it with his needle-sharp teeth so that it lost its voice and was no more fun. Over the next two days a purple pig and an unknown species of creature with horns met the same fate.

Grandma wondered what on earth he was going to do with himself in his spare time, but since there was obviously no possibility of training him to do the vacuuming or anything useful of that kind, he would just have to stare into space or go to sleep. So it was: and as long as he had gourmet food, a good walk every day and plenty of fuss he was perfectly content.

🕮

When you take on a dog you really don't know what you are getting into, especially if it has had a previous life. Pippy's worst failing by far, hinted at by Janet the kennel-maid, is his behaviour with other dogs. He just cannot get on peacefully with them. No dog is too large or too small for him to challenge. No dog is too fierce, no dog too inoffensive. Even lady dogs are fair game. Chivalry has no meaning for him.

I shouldn't really make light of it. A dog fight is about the worst thing you can imagine, an absolute horror. So whenever another dog appears on the horizon and Pippy begins his slow stalking routine, we run after him and pick him up, to avoid a dreadful scene. He always has to be carried past the farm gate for the protection of Sam's placid old collie Ned, who is politely baffled by his ferocious snarling.

We found a book in the travelling library one day with the optimistic title, *Let Your Dog Know Who's Boss*. It made frequent reference to the Jack Russell terrier, "a small dog which thinks it's big". Many Jack Russells are utterly reckless and will tackle anything, warned the book, and went on to

suggest various training methods which all sounded like hard work. Grandma looked at Pippy over her spectacles and spoke to him severely.

"Pippy, you should be grateful that we didn't read this book before we got you, or we might have changed our minds."

I think he *is* grateful, although on his walks he doesn't show it. At home he is comfortable among us and seems like an honorary human, but in the great outdoors he is one hundred per cent dog, absorbed in his natural surroundings and only distantly aware of the rest of the family. He trots ahead of us with an occasional hop-and-skip, stopping here and there to investigate interesting smells, and only breaking into a run if a rabbit or squirrel needs chasing. Usually he picks up the scent rather than seeing the animal itself: he can't see very far ahead because his face is so near the ground. Once we walked for about ten minutes along a narrow stony track between high banks, preceded by a brazenly bold black cat. Pippy, head down, followed the scent faithfully but never once looked up to see the cat strolling along in front. The cat finally grew tired of waiting to be chased and disappeared through the hedge.

Holes in the ground are another of Pippy's interests. However, we have noticed that he only puts his nose in and doesn't follow it. *Let Your Dog Know Who's Boss* taught us the curious fact that Jack Russell terriers sometimes become stuck in fox-holes or rabbit-holes and, like Winnie-the-Pooh, have to wait to grow thinner before they can escape. Did that happen once to Pippy, without the benefit of anyone to read a sustaining book to him? We shall probably never know. He remains, as Grandpa says, a Dog of Mystery.

But apart from his bad manners with other dogs and frequent failure to come when called, Pippy is well-behaved and mostly quite humble. He has no desire to go upstairs – upstairs being firmly associated in his mind with baths – so he doesn't sneak up there and try sleeping on the beds, as some dogs might. He doesn't steal food from the pantry or chew Grandma's knitting. However, there are times when he tries to get above himself, and being a wise dog he knows that Grandma, rather than Grandpa, is the person to be worked on.

One morning last Easter holidays I got out of bed early and went downstairs in my dressing-gown to fetch a book. The previous one, *The Thirteenth Hour*, which I had only started the day before, had been so gripping that I had been forced to finish it under the bedclothes by torch-light. At the bottom of the stairs I heard Grandma in the living room laying the fire, and put my head round the door to say hello. To my surprise, Grandma looked up guiltily from the hearth and put her finger to her lips.

"Let's just pretend we haven't seen him," she whispered, glancing across at her armchair, where Pippy the Innocent Dog lay sweetly curled up as though by right, giving every appearance of untroubled sleep. I sat down on my sawn-off log in the inglenook and watched him closely while Grandma swept the hearth and the rug, but he continued to breathe deeply and convincingly.

"I think Grandpa's coming down," I said, hearing his footsteps along the passage upstairs. Grandma turned round and looked with a shocked expression at Pippy as if she had just noticed him for the first time.

"You bad pup! Out of that chair!" she cried in a scandalised squeak. He opened his eyes and looked at her reproachfully, but made no other movement. Grandma dropped her voice by about three octaves. "Come on, out!" she growled, rattling the dustpan at him and trying to sound like someone who wouldn't take "No" for an answer. Pippy edged forwards an inch or two.

"Come on, you naughty dog – down!" said Grandma in an urgent hiss now, hearing Grandpa on the stairs. I jumped up and pulled hard on Pippy's collar, and he finally dropped to the floor, not showing the least sign of repentance. He stepped into his box bed under the settle with an injured sigh, while Grandma hastily brushed the chair with the carpet brush. When Grandpa came in he was surprised to see me up so early, but nothing else out of the ordinary met his eye.

Grandma sympathises with Pippy for having his bed on the floor. She thinks it might be a bit cold sometimes, even under the settle. But I know what Grandpa would say.

"He's a dog! He's got a fur coat!"

Grandpa is adamant that a dog is happier if it knows its place, and I think he is probably right.

Of course, even the best-behaved dog may sometimes be led astray by temptation, especially if the temptation is an edible one.

One day this summer, a couple of weeks into my stay, Grandma and I were to have a special lunch outing to town. The early afternoon bus back from town doesn't go through the villages, but straight along the top road, so the plan was that Grandpa would come in Lucy and collect us from the bus stop there a little after three o'clock.

Before we set off in the morning, I explained to Pippy that we were going on a "not for dogs" expedition and gave him some of his favourite treat, cheese cut into small cubes, so that he would have pleasant things to remember while we were out.

We waited for about twenty minutes at the bus stop on the corner of Vicarage Lane, and began to wonder if both our watches were wrong, since no-one else was there. Then, just as hope was fading, we saw to our astonishment a *double-decker* bus swaying into view at the top of the village and bearing down on us. Curious cottage windows opened, and Mrs Studley came out of the Post Office Stores to see what Old Tom thought of it. The conductress standing on the platform at the back just rolled her eyes and said they'd had trouble at the depot. To my great joy there was hardly anyone on the bus, and the long front seat upstairs was vacant. We sat down on it for a grandstand view.

A double-decker bus is an incongruous thing in a country lane. We rode through villages at a dizzying height, staring down into private gardens and buffeting the treetops alarmingly. We enjoyed a superior view of familiar landmarks such as the ugly brick police house with the blue lamp over the door, the house where the old lady with fifty cats lives, and the row of cottages with the stream through their gardens and hump-backed bridges to their front doors. We towered over untidy hedges and high banks full of brambles,

ragwort, bindweed and nettles, which may or may not have had an old stone wall buried somewhere in their midst. We brushed roughly past the bracken that grows along the edge of the common. And on the outskirts of town we travelled along the rows of identical brick houses at eaves level and gawped shamelessly into their upstairs windows.

The conductress didn't come up to take our fares until we were nearly there. She wore a black trouser suit, which seemed very modern and fashionable to me, and a spotted headscarf, which spoilt the effect a little. Grandma asked for one and one-half returns, and the conductress wound the handle of the ticket machine that she carried on a leather strap over her shoulder and tore off two pink paper tickets.

The bus dropped us in the High Street, near the old lady who plays the squeeze-box in front of the Town Hall. Grandma always gives her some money, and lives in hope that she will learn to play it properly. We went into the ironmonger's first, to collect the fire tongs from being mended, before stepping into the big department store for lunch.

The department store is an elegant place with high ceilings, crystal chandeliers and fluted columns decorated with greenery. You can glide to the upper floor by escalator and return in a lift lined with mirrors. Lunch in the restaurant starts off a bit like school dinner – two perfectly round blobs of mashed potato with the meat, and a mere dribble of gravy – but to follow there is Knickerbocker Glory in a tall glass with a long spoon, and of course no washing up.

At the park we spent ten minutes patiently working free the two swings, which had been turned over and over until their chains were in knots and their seats almost out of reach. I'm too old for the slide and roundabout now, so when I had had enough of swinging we strolled over to the pavilion and watched white-clad ladies and gentlemen playing bowls on grass as smooth as Miss Winterton's green Wilton carpet.

The bus home was very late. Grandma kept wondering whether to run up the street and ring Grandpa from the call box by the Town Hall, but the bus might not wait for her, and anyway Grandpa was probably in the garden and wouldn't hear the telephone ringing. The bus finally arrived,

just an ordinary single-decker this time, and made no effort to make up the lost half-hour. Grandpa would have a long wait, but he would wait on and not give up, that we knew. When we reached our stop on the top road at twenty to four, there was Lucy in the lay-by with Grandpa inside reading. He got out and walked round to open the passenger door for us, with *Journey to the Centre of the Earth* still open in his hand.

"Lurch, you are worth your weight in gold!" cried Grandma; but Grandpa seemed distracted and didn't respond in character.

"I don't suppose a dog would eat *After Eight* mints, would it?" he said as he got back in his seat and handed his book to Grandma to look after. "I can't for the life of me remember putting the box away. I just had one or two after my lunch, to console me in my loneliness, you know." He started the engine and turned cautiously out onto the road.

Grandma refrained from any remarks on the undoubted decadence of eating *After Eight* mints in the middle of the day, and said she didn't think they would be Pippy's cup of tea.

"He wouldn't be able to get them out of their wrappers," I added.

But as soon as we walked into the kitchen we knew we were wrong. Pippy the Remorseful Dog had heard Lucy drive into the yard and was already sliding towards us across the lino on his elbows, writhing in apology and smiling his most ingratiating smile, his ears flat to his head and his eyes great saucers of guilt.

"Oh, Pippy, what have you done?" asked Grandma. Grandma is never very good at sounding stern, but Pippy's conscience-stricken tail thumped the floor, and his demeanour grew more abject still.

"It was my fault – an irresistible temptation," said Grandpa, stepping gingerly into the living room and round the end of the settle. Yes, there on the floor near the window lay the dark green box, overturned and empty. Scattered about were the mints, all half-removed from their little black envelopes, all nibbled but none of them consumed.

Before us there rose the vision of a small dog all alone, very fond of chocolate but not at all keen on mint filling, dipping an exploratory tooth

into each dark square in the hope that it might taste better than the last. Poor Pippy! He had tried every single one and found them all the same.

This naughtiness paled in comparison with the antics of my school-friend Jennifer's collie, Ringo, who had twice made off with the Sunday joint. All the same, a firm rebuke was essential. We needed someone who could banish Pippy to his bed in a shocked but commanding tone, and who could pick up all the mints and their wrappers with disapproving noises and not so much as the ghost of a smile. It was clear to Grandma and to me that Grandpa was that someone, so we fled and left him to it. He may have heard muffled laughter coming from the kitchen as he went about his melancholy task.

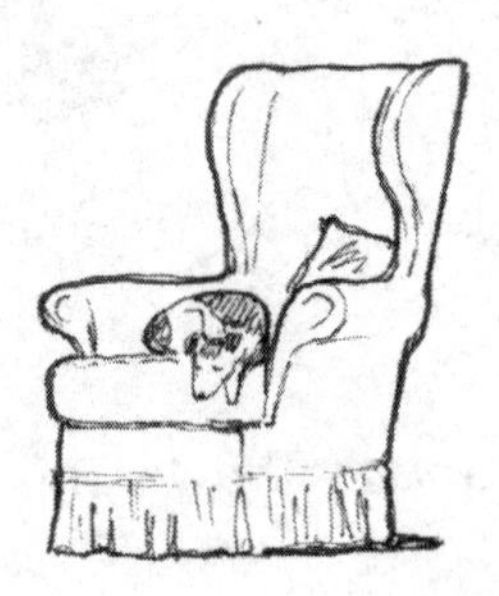

Chapter Nine
IN PRAISE OF RAIN

A very wet day – enthusiasm of Grandma for same – I make my own entertainment – the gramophone – the sewing machine – the Val Doonican Show

IT was a Saturday morning. Grandma and I were lingering over our breakfast cups of tea, and rather unkindly letting Grandpa wash up by himself. The garden side of the house basked in brilliant sun, but the sky over the yard was dark. "Black as a bag!" said Grandma, gleefully.

Grandma is so fond of rain that once, when it started after a long dry spell, I saw her go out into the yard and dance in it – not a wild dance but a genteel sort of waltz with an imaginary partner. Her favourite thing in the world is sitting by the fire while rain falls on the garden. Thunderstorms send her into ecstasies.

"We'd better take the pup up the lane before the heavens open," said Grandma. Pippy, who had been snoozing on the hearthrug while we sipped our tea, sat up on hearing "the pup" and began watching us keenly with his ears well forward. The minute we put down our cups and

pushed our chairs back, he was on his feet and skidding across the room to the hall doorway. He leapt around and got in my way while I tried to open the door, then flew over the step into the hall and jumped ever more wildly up and down in the confined space while we climbed into our wellingtons and searched along the row of hanging coats for some suitable rainwear. I found my anorak, and Grandma unfolded a rain hat and tied it under her chin, put on her long mackintosh and took a giant black umbrella from the stand.

We then began on the usual struggle to attach Pippy to his lead. He jumped up, lay down, rolled over, chewed the lead and even nipped my hand, but without hurting, then went through the whole process again in case he had missed anything out. Finally I managed to clip the lead onto his collar and we got out into the yard. The tree by the outhouse was sharply lit against a lowering greenish sky, but no rain was falling yet.

A Jack Russell terrier is a great scent-follower, and Pippy couldn't wait to get outside into the lane and start investigating the banks. He dragged me to the gate, preferring strangulation to delay, his tail spinning like a propeller. Once we were out through the gate I let him off his lead. From the way he had been straining at it, you would have expected him to spring forward as if released from a starting gate, but no, he just padded up the lane a few paces ahead of us, sniffing the ground rapturously.

The sky overhead was growing darker every minute. When we were some way up the lane, big drops began to fall.

"Marvellous," said Grandma. "Let's get the brolly up."

We walked on, and as we walked the rain pattered harder and harder on the umbrella. Soon it was drumming. But every time we passed under a tree the umbrella was suddenly silent. There was a good smell of newly soaked soil, and of dust being washed away. Tree branches dripped, and the tarmac road gleamed darkly. Only the bedraggled Pippy seemed unimproved by being out in this glorious downpour.

"I think Pippy's had enough," said Grandma presently. "Let's turn round."

Rivulets of water flowed past us down each side of the lane as we walked back, dragging long stalks of grass into the current and trying to uproot them from the sodden banks. When we reached home, the kitchen light was on and we could see Grandpa still at the sink, too deep in thought to notice us coming back. "Bless him," said Grandma. "What would we do without him?"

"Wipe your feet!" I instructed Pippy, holding him firmly and dragging his paws across the door mat one by one. I always say the words in the faint hope that he may learn their meaning and one day wipe his feet on command.

After I had unhooked his towel from the back of the door and given him a rub down, he shook himself, took a quick drink of water and headed straight for the fireside to clean his paws properly.

Grandpa had finished the washing up and was now giving the sink a thorough scrub with Vim. He appreciates rain because the garden needs it, but he doesn't like being cooped up indoors for too long. He asked me what I was going to do all day.

Grandpa always thinks I will be bored here when it's raining, but I very rarely am. Even when I was quite small and staying here with Mum, I found plenty to do by myself – which was surprising in view of the shortage of toys in Grandma's house. Most of Mum's childhood things had disappeared, and Grandma couldn't think what had happened to them. The china dolls, the wooden hoop, the whip-and-top, and others long forgotten, were all gone, and the only survivors, apart from Mum's old bear who lives at our house, were the roller skates, the skipping rope and a metal clockwork robin with nearly all the paint rubbed off and the key missing.

But Grandma often used to buy me little plastic nothings from the Post Office Stores, and besides, there were plenty of unofficial things to play with – such as Grandma's cracked ivory fan, the silver concertina napkin rings which could be expanded into crowns big enough for my head, and the china figurines of ladies in swirling dresses on the end room mantelpiece, which I was allowed to take down and look at as long

as I kept them on the carpet. And among the interesting objects on the sideboard in the living room there was a strange varnished coconut, which had patterns carved on its dark shiny surface by sailors, and smelt old and foreign.

Sometimes I used to tidy Grandma's sewing box for her, or arrange the buttons from the button box in patterns on the floor, or sit at Grandma's dressing-table putting on wobbly lipstick and rearranging the scent bottles. The dressing-table has a large mirror fixed to it with two extra hinged pieces at the sides; by swinging them to the correct angle I could get a most interesting view of my own profile, or even the back of my head.

In the living room there is a cylindrical pouffe, which is supposed to be for people in armchairs to prop their feet up on. This pouffe is now rather threadbare and out of shape, having had heavy use over the years as a piece of circus equipment. I have never been to a real circus, but I have seen them on television, and when I was about seven, I was thrilled to discover that I could turn Grandma's pouffe onto its side, stand on it and, with practice, make it roll around the room exactly like the circus performer's drum. If I walked forwards the pouffe went backwards, and if I walked backwards it went forwards – rather unevenly, it's true, but Grandma was impressed.

My attempt to give myself a brown face in order to become an indoor pirate was less successful. I had read a *Topsy and Tim* book in which the twins acquired richly polished dark complexions using nothing but cocoa powder and water, but after a smeary session at Grandma's kitchen table with pale brown liquid dripping down my neck, I can testify that this does not work.

The indoor pirate did, however, after a few catastrophic false starts, make a very pleasing treasure map by burning the edges of the paper in the fire. He had a wonderfully piratical scarf, a black silk eye-patch and an earring made of a brass curtain ring hung round his ear with invisible thread. Grandma had no gold doubloons or pieces of eight, but she let

me borrow the next best thing, her two precious George V crowns, even bigger than half-crowns and twice as heavy.

A whole wet day or even two could be devoted to making a house for a jelly baby to live in. A jelly baby house only has an indoors, never an outdoors. From outside it looks exactly like a shoe-box, which is what it is, but inside it has windows with views cut out of magazines, framed by pleated curtains that run stiffly on string curtain-rails; it has furniture made out of cotton reels and matchboxes, carpets of felt, rugs of fur and even hand-patterned wallpaper. The resident jelly baby lies on its matchbox bed in the midst of all this splendour for a week or more, gathering dust, and is then given a quick wipe and eaten.

One wet afternoon years ago Grandma taught me to knit remnants of wool into squares. I still knit a couple more on each visit, and some far-off day I shall sew them all together into a rug. Sometimes I knit at home, but it never lasts long because Mum can't repair the holes the way Grandma does.

It was probably a wet day when Grandpa showed me how to make a flick-book. You can do it in a notebook or in the corner of a drawing book. On the bottom page you draw a stick man, then on the page above you draw him again, but with his hand slightly lifted. This is easy, because you can see the original man through the paper. So you go on, until you have drawn the man in a slightly different position on every page. Then you riffle through the book for the highly rewarding experience of seeing him raise his hat and put it back on again.

You can, of course, while away many a happy hour drawing round people in the *Radio Times* with a biro. You just outline the face, body, eyes, mouth and so on, and then add glasses, jewellery, beard, horns – whatever takes your fancy. Most of the pictures are masterpieces (you never knew you could draw so well!) and the paper crinkles delightfully.

Sometimes I leaf through Grandma's photograph album. She only has one, and there aren't many pictures in it compared with the number most people take nowadays. The earliest photos are in sepia, showing formal groups of severe-looking people in Victorian clothes. Then comes one of

Grandpa aged three in a sailor suit, with hand-tinted blue eyes and pink cheeks, and someone's wedding picture in which Grandma appears as a bridesmaid with long ringlets and an unrecognisably serious face. There follow two pages of seaside postcards with rude cartoons and captions on them. I like to prise them out of the corners that hold them, and look at the old postage stamps and the illegible messages in old-fashioned handwriting on their backs.

A whole page of the album is given over to a studio portrait of Grandpa as a young man, looking a bit like David Niven; then comes Grandma and Grandpa's wedding photograph, with all the guests in dark coats and sensible shoes. They all have rather grim expressions, but Grandma says it was a cold day. The next few pages are crookedly stuck with blurred snapshots of Mum at various ages and in no particular order – riding a tricycle with huge wheels and thin tyres, modelling a gymslip, grinning up at a budgie on her head. There is also a picture of Grandma, Grandpa and a smallish Mum walking along a wind-swept promenade – obviously taken by an obliging passer-by – and then Grandpa appears in his wartime ARP warden's uniform in the town where they used to live, this time looking like Mr Hodges in *Dad's Army*, but more benign.

The last few pages of the album contain more recent colour snaps, taken on Grandma's Green Shield Stamp camera. They are mostly of me on the beach or holding Pippy in the garden, and you can guess the year by the length of my legs. The slightly sinister pink shadows across the top corners of some of these pictures are caused by Grandma forgetting that she shouldn't hold the camera with her finger obscuring the lens, and me not reminding her in time.

Of course there are days at Grandma's when boredom does set in and all I can think of is to turn on the television, but it's usually the test card. One memorable wet Saturday at home when the *Radio Times* said cricket, I switched on at random and was electrified to hear a silky voice purring, "Last night I dreamt I went to Manderley again…" I called out to Mum, and she came and watched it with me.

Such magic may never be repeated, but I live in hope.

Grandma is always free for "activities" on wet afternoons when she has finished her chores and changed her clothes. We play cards or board games, and sometimes I can even persuade her to try some artwork. I ask her to draw something – a dog or a horse, perhaps, and she always says, "Oh, heavens, I couldn't possibly draw *that!*" But then she will gamely attempt it anyway, which is fun to watch, and if the final result is at all recognisable we get quite excited.

I often play the wind-up gramophone in the living room on rainy days. On the bottom shelf of its cabinet and on the floor underneath there are stacks of "78" records in tattered brown paper covers with bent-over corners. Each one has only a few minutes of music on it, and playing them is quite a skill. First you wind the handle on the side of the gramophone. Then you put the record on the turntable, slide a lever to start it going round, and lift up the heavy arm with the needle on the end, being careful to place the needle in just the right groove without letting it jump off the edge. At this stage you need not just skill, but some courage, because the record is spinning recklessly fast, more than twice as fast as the long-playing ones I'm used to at home, and the needle rasps so harshly in the groove when it first touches it that you hardly dare set it down. However, once the music starts it sounds all right, and you get used to ignoring the scratches.

Some of the records are piano concertos and symphonies, but no-one except Grandpa listens to those, because you have to be pretty keen to keep getting up to turn them over. The ones I play are the old music hall songs – "Sarah sitting in the shoe-shine shop", "Whose Izzy is he?", or my favourite one, "Over the garden wall", which is about cats howling but has a good tune. When I play them Grandma may come in from the kitchen in her pinny, with the potato peeler in one hand and a half-peeled potato in the other, to hum along and tap her foot. After a while the

gramophone begins to run down – the beat drags, the carefree tenor beomes a serious baritone – and I have to leap up and wind the handle on the side to get it going again.

📖

"Well, this rain's set in and no mistake!" declared Martha the scullery maid, rinsing out the cloth and giving the taps a final wipe. "What are you going to do with yourself?" added Grandpa in his own voice, still convinced I should die of boredom. "You can't type all day."

But I already had a plan.

"Grandma, you know when we did the spring cleaning and we found some of the left-over material from the blue dress you made me for my birthday, and you said perhaps you could make a bag to go with it some time? Could you do it now, so I could help?"

"Well now, that's a very good idea," said Grandma. "There couldn't be a better day for it."

I followed her into the corn cupboard.

"Yes," she said, half to herself, as she turned over bundles of cloth in the drawer. "That frock is very becoming. A bit of a bag to go with it would be nice."

Making that exquisite quilted bag took Grandma all day. I had never watched her sewing before, and I could not have imagined how long it would take, or how neat it would be. I felt important sitting next to her at the sewing machine and seeing the bag take shape as she turned it inside out and right way out again, over and over, so carefully, getting every line of stitching perfectly straight and checking it after each little burst of sewing, even spending nearly an hour making an inside pocket. Her foot worked the treadle, one hand went up at intervals to turn the wheel on the side of the machine, and she held the pins in her mouth between tight lips. I handed her the scissors when they were needed, and picked up the pins that dropped every now and then to the floor. Outside, the rain streamed down and dripped relentlessly off the eaves. Absorbed in what we were doing, we scarcely spoke a word.

Grandpa left the papers he was working on at his bureau and made us a beautiful lunch of scrambled egg on toast with the crusts removed; then Grandma went back to her sewing and I settled down to some typing at the dining table. Pippy positioned himself under the table as a footstool, so that I could rub his back with my stockinged feet, and Grandpa made up the fire for us before setting off for the greenhouse to see to his geranium cuttings.

The bag was finished just as the clock struck four. I had the blue dress with me, so I went to put it on and modelled the bag with it, twirling round the room and popping and unpopping the press-stud on the flap. Grandpa, warming his chilled hands by the fire, was full of praise: he never ceases to be impressed by Grandma's sewing. He declared me a "first-class bobby-dazzler". I put a cardigan on over the blue dress and helped Grandpa get the tea ready while Grandma put her machine away. Since we had only had a light lunch, we wheeled in a heavy tea trolley, laden with bread-and-butter, plum jam, cold ham, home-pickled onions, tiny jars of meat paste, chocolate finger biscuits and the remains of another sponge cake, rather dry. And, of course, the teapot.

Over the remains of tea, Grandpa read aloud the latest episode of *Three Men in a Boat.*

Still it rained. Grandma got an umbrella and took Pippy up the lane again for a change of scene while Grandpa and I did the washing up. Then Grandma washed her hair and came down with her curlers in for the night.

Unlike Mum, who always has her hair set at the hairdresser's and sits under a hairdryer like a huge pink helmet, Grandma prefers the old-fashioned way. Sometimes I borrow Grandma's curlers and have a go with them myself. They are hard and lumpy to sleep in, and the pins stick into my head. Usually half the rollers fall out during the night

and I wake up with one side of my hair flat and the other side sticking out sideways in such unflattering corkscrew shapes that I have to wash it again and put it back to normal before I can go out in public. Grandma never seems to have this problem.

We all agreed that there was only one way to end such a deluge of a day: watch *The Val Doonican Show* and have an early night with hot water bottles.

"How are you enjoying your colour television set at home?" asked Grandma. "It must be nice to see what colour Val's sweaters are."

"Oh yes! And the Virginian wears a red shirt, you know. I always used to think it was grey."

"Well, of all things!"

Val sat in his rocking chair with his sleeves rolled up, singing with his gentle smile, "Walk tall, walk straight and look the world right in the eye. That's what my mother told me, when I was about knee-high." He seemed to be singing just for us.

Chapter Ten
THE SECRET PLAN

The romantic ruin – unfortunate disappearance of small dog – the ruin loses its charm – small dog discovered in grand surroundings – magnanimity of Grandma

THE rain spent most of Sunday blowing itself away. Monday brought warm sunshine and a light breeze, as a wash-day should always try to do, and I decided that the time had come to carry out my secret plan.

The plan had first crept into my mind on one of our "motoring" expeditions into the hills. Grandpa had brought us back by an adventurous route, along a lane with grass growing down the middle, whose high banks were so overgrown it was almost impassable. Lucy bumped and shuddered in and out of potholes, which caused her engine to stall more than once, and Grandma began to worry that the lane would be a dead end and we should have to back out. But Grandpa assured her that he knew exactly where we were, and to prove it he predicted that in a couple of minutes we would pass the gates of Biddlecombe Hall.

Now that was a funny thing, said Grandma, because Mrs Studley had been talking about Biddlecombe Hall just the other day, and saying what a shame it was. What a shame what was? I asked from the back seat.

"It's been a shell for years, and now they want to demolish it," said Grandma. "Mrs Studley says it was a beautiful place, before it burnt down."

Grandpa said he had read all about it in the local paper. "It could have been repaired if they hadn't left it so long," he said. "Now some builder chappie wants to knock it down and build twenty new houses. Twenty! Of course then they'll be all for widening this lane, and heaven knows what else. These people are the limit."

Grandpa is at his most cantankerous on the subject of "development". Grandma patiently points out to him that he has a very nice house in a nice place, and that other people would like one as well, but he still thinks they should be put somewhere else. In his exasperation he stalled Lucy's engine again.

"Don't bother starting up," said Grandma. "This is it, by the looks of it."

Lucy had kangaroo-hopped to a halt in front of a pair of ivy-covered gate pillars about seven feet high. Leaning back from them were two tall, rusted wrought-iron gates, one of them off its hinges and supported only by the overgrown shrubbery behind. A gravel drive, green with weeds, led away out of sight. No house was visible from the road.

We all got out of the car, closed the doors and let the quiet settle upon us. Even Pippy seemed awed by the hush, and by the decaying splendour of those gates. He sat down in front of them and put his head on one side, as if expecting some apparition to come forth from the dark depths of the drive.

I was desperate to go in and see the ruined house, and I knew that Mum would have been in there like a shot, but Grandma said it would be trespassing. It wasn't like Grandma to put a damper on things, but Grandpa seemed to agree with her and I sensed there was no point in arguing. That was when my secret plan began to form.

When we got home I found Grandpa's Ordnance Survey map and plotted a route to Biddlecombe Hall going by way of the knoll. Then I waited.

When the day came, I was still unsure whether I would carry out my plan or not. Concealing it from Grandma didn't feel quite right, so I tried to justify it by convincing myself that it probably wouldn't happen.

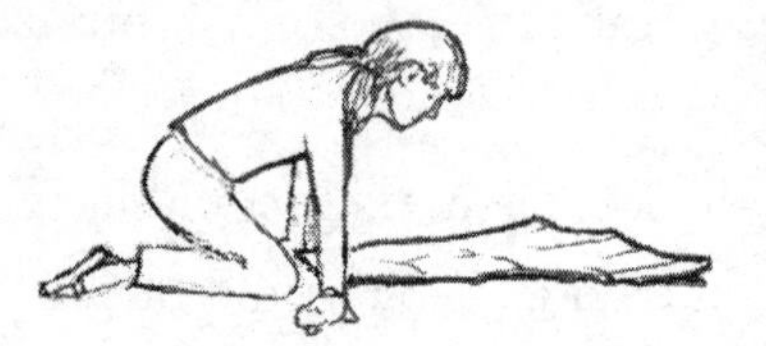

I told Grandma that it was such a lovely morning Pippy and I were going to the knoll by ourselves, which was partly true at any rate. I packed a rucksack with a flask of cold water, Grandpa's map, a block of fruit-and-nut chocolate and a handful of dog biscuits, and promised to be back for dinner at one o'clock.

The knoll is one of my favourite places. Halfway to the top, there is an old stone bench partly buried in the ground, and near the bench stands a tall, straight beech tree with a rope hanging from its lowest bough, on which I like to swing in the style of Tarzan, Robin Hood or my latest hero, Rudolf Rassendyll of *The Prisoner of Zenda.*

In imitation of the dashing Rudolf I have also taught myself to raise one eyebrow quizzically. In case you are interested, the way to master this skill is to lie awake for a whole night, holding down one eyebrow while you repeatedly raise the other. By morning, quizzicality will have been achieved.

Today Pippy wasn't disposed to linger while I swung, and Grandma wasn't there to keep hold of him, so I climbed straight on up to the top of the hill. As I strode over its gently domed summit, Pippy scampered about and jumped over tree roots and rocks: it reminded me of *The Horse of the Year Show* on television.

We were approaching the far side of the knoll, beyond the furthest point I had explored with Grandma. I slackened my pace, and wondered if we were going to go to Biddlecombe Hall or not. Perhaps I would just have a look at the view from the other side and then decide whether to turn back or go on.

But I couldn't see a view from the far side. The woods seemed to have changed their character, as if this part had a different owner. The tree cover was so dense that hardly any sky showed through. Everything was shades of green; even the brown and grey were shades of green. The trees all had ivy growing up them, and there were a great many fallen ones which had been left to rot where they lay. Some of them had branches which had continued growing upwards from the horizontal trunk and become trees in their own right. All about the place were dead leaves, moss, decomposing logs, and scraps of barbed wire fence poking out of the mud. I had to walk at the very edge of the path, if path it could be called, and sometimes on fallen branches. Although I tested them first, some still collapsed under my weight and let me down into the mud with a squelch. My lace-up shoes were stout, but not stout enough for this. Pippy's usual skill at keeping clean had failed him and he was caked up to his elbows.

We reached the bottom of the hill and scrambled through the last piece of straggly barbed wire into an open field. From here we could be at Biddlecombe Hall in about ten minutes. I looked out across the field and back up at the knoll, and decided that Biddlecombe Hall would be a good place to eat our elevenses. It seemed we were going there after all.

Pippy trotted close to my heel in a friendly way as I followed the line of the hedge along one field and the next. I put him temporarily on his lead while I went over the stile into the lane and he went under – just in case there might be any hazards on the other side such as passing traffic or dogs. But the lane was deserted.

The gates to the Hall were almost opposite the stile. Pippy, no longer awe-struck, went straight in. After a dramatic pause, I followed. I was the heroine of *Rebecca,* he was the dog Jasper.

I expected the drive to wind on and on, this way and that, but at the end of one long right-hand curve, where the drive petered out into a wide space all grown over with tree saplings and thistles, Biddlecombe Hall came into view.

It was a large, square house, once solid but hollow now, like a stage set with no substance. It certainly wasn't Manderley, but it was quite a respectable ruin all the same – not like the rather boring abbey I went round with Mum and Dad on holiday, which just had its foundations and a few fragments of wall standing. Biddlecombe Hall had full-height stone walls with spindly trees growing close against them, both inside and out. It had staring gaps where once there had been windows. It even had the charred remains of a roof.

My plan had worked – this was a true adventure!

While Pippy chewed some long grass I climbed the front steps, and through the hole where the door should have been I saw the skeleton of a staircase and a cage of blackened ceiling rafters poised precariously above. I longed to go inside, but I could hear Grandma's voice in my head saying it wasn't sensible. The roof or the floor might fall in at any moment. I obeyed the voice and instead paced slowly all round the outside of the house, stopping on tiptoe to look in through the window holes, and trying to imagine what each room would have been used for.

I was sure this couldn't be trespassing. The gates hadn't been locked or boarded up. There were no threatening signs saying "Trespassers will be prosecuted." I felt justified in coming, and proud of my daring. I was a witness of history. How sad to think that one day soon, in place of this glamorous relic, there would be a smooth tarmac road called "Biddlecombe Close" or "Knoll View", and twenty brick houses like the ones in Vicarage Lane, with unfenced front gardens and baby willow trees.

At the back of the house there was a terrace with a stone balustrade, looking over an expanse of rough grass. Ivy and brambles had worked their way between the stones and loosened them so that the balustrade had fallen away in places; some of the paving slabs were tilted up from the ground and lay all at angles like the old graves in the churchyard.

Elevenses were forgotten. I half-closed my eyes and imagined I saw a smooth-shaved lawn where now there was a neglected field. Instead of clumps of bracken I saw strutting peacocks, turning and fanning their gorgeous swaying tails. Adorning the back of the house I pictured neatly

tumbling roses and clematis instead of dusty thickets of ivy and thirty-foot brambles. Down the middle of the lawn were two rows of conifers – yew trees, I thought, because they looked the same as the ones in the churchyard. They might once have been clipped into an elegant, well-spaced avenue of cones or spirals, but now they had almost met together into one long, dark, shaggy hedge.

The bark of a dog from somewhere in the woods beyond the old lawn startled me out of my dreams, and I realised I had not seen or thought about Pippy for some time. Was that him, chasing squirrels? I called, but there was only silence. I ran into the trees and called several more times, as loudly as I dared. There was no response.

Now I did feel like a trespasser. I plodded back through the wood and across the grass, imagining myself watched all the way. I crept round the outside of the house one more time, calling Pippy in a voice that was not much more than a hoarse whisper, and hoping at every moment to see him emerging from a thicket, or standing on a window ledge, or lying in the shade by the front steps.

The ruined house looked bleak now, all its mysterious charm frozen. I wished there *were* twenty nice ordinary houses there, with people in their front gardens watering roses or washing cars, who would offer me the use of their telephone and who would sympathise and tell me about the time *their* dog disappeared, so I wouldn't feel so bad.

I looked at my watch and saw that I must be setting off home, with or without Pippy, or I would be late for dinner and Grandma would wonder where I had got to.

I ran back down the drive and out into the lane, wishing I knew how to do one of those piercing whistles. Poor Pippy – he had probably chased something and then lost himself. Was he looking for me as I was looking for him? Perhaps he would go up to someone and they would read his name-disc and ring up Grandma. Perhaps he would be waiting for me when I got back to the house, and all would be well. I wished I deserved it. Trespassing or no trespassing, it was clear to me now that I

had quite deliberately told Grandma a lie, and it was a terrible thought. Turning back into the lane I began jogging homewards on feet of lead.

It was one o'clock by the time I arrived at the top of our lane, and there was still a long way to go. I was out of breath and the flask in my rucksack was digging into my back. But as I staggered round the last bend of the lane I saw a hopeful sight: Grandma came out of the gate, caught sight of me, and waved a piece of paper. I waved back and broke into a weary trot, and Grandma came to meet me. I saw that she had put her face on although it was before lunch – another good sign.

"A lady called Mrs Cunningham has just rung. She's got Pippy. She found him in her garden. What a good thing you've come back! We were just going to come and look for you."

I was so relieved I laughed at the thought of a search party being sent out for me as well.

"She lives quite a way off," continued Grandma, as we walked back into the yard together. "We'd better get over there immediately or she'll think we're not bothered. Dinner will just have to wait and keep warm. Here is Lurch, our trusty driver."

Lurch was closing the garage doors after bringing Lucy out, and permitting himself a few grumpy remarks. But in the car I shared out the fruit-and-nut chocolate from my rucksack and he cheered up at once.

"I would never have thought Pippy could get so far on those little legs of his," mused Grandma. "And it's odd for him to get lost and run off from a place he knows so well."

I gulped, and cleared my throat to deliver my confession from the back seat. I felt like a child in one of those pious moral tales, who strays from the right path and has to be Taught a Lesson.

"Er, Grandma, we weren't – "

"But I'm sure he won't ever do it again," interrupted Grandma, changing her tone but still looking straight ahead of her along the tree-shadowed road.

"No, he certainly won't!" I replied with feeling. And that was that – no more was said. Grandma never did like those pious moral tales.

Mrs Cunningham's house was easy to find: she had given Grandma good directions. We felt rather incongruous creeping along the winding gravel drive in Lucy. This was like Biddlecombe Hall brought back to life. The gravel was weed-free, the shrubbery billowing but under control. The yew hedge by the house was so neat it looked as though it had been carved out rather than clipped. The drive swept round an immaculate circular lawn in front of the house, and yellow roses climbed the columns of a square stone porch. A pair of peacock-shaped bushes in white pots flanked the front steps.

"Well," said Grandpa, "that dog certainly has good taste."

At one side of the drive, in front of a coach-house with a bell-tower on its roof, there stood a resplendent green Bentley gleaming in the sun. Grandma suggested to Grandpa that he ought to park well away from it, whether because she thought he might hit it or because she thought Lucy would not appear to advantage next to such magnificence, I don't know. Probably both.

Having tucked Lucy in alongside the rhododendrons on the other side of the drive, Grandpa settled down to study the map while Grandma and I got out and approached the front door. I could tell Grandma was preparing an explanation, but it was unnecessary. Before we had a chance to ring the bell, the door was opened by a tall lady in a polka-dot dress with sunglasses on top of her head.

"My dears, how worried you must have been about your adorable little dog! Isn't he a pet? Do come in." She reached out to shake hands with Grandma. "I'm Jean Cunningham – delighted to meet you. Do come through, won't you? He's out at the back – very dirty and tired, poor little lamb, but none the worse otherwise. Malcolm, my husband, is about the place somewhere. Men always disappear just when they're wanted, don't they? Malcolm!" she called upstairs to the gallery as we passed underneath.

We came out through glass doors onto a wide stone terrace. Set into it at one end was a very blue swimming pool, and near the edge of the pool lay a familiar-looking small dog, tied to a striped sun-lounger and taking advantage of the shade it provided. There was a bowl of water near him, also thoughtfully placed in the shade. He had heard our approach, and was drumming his tail on the ground in his best ingratiating manner, ears well back. He had cleaned his front paws but given up on the rest of his appearance.

"Pippy, you naughty dog," said Grandma sternly, "come here!" Pippy's tail thumped but he didn't move.

"Oh, he's exhausted, the poor little angel," cooed Mrs Cunningham, bending down to pat his head. "Don't be hard on him – who knows what he may have been through? We've quite fallen in love with him! Are you sure you wouldn't like a new home for him?" she added, playfully. She offered us drinks, and we really had to accept for politeness' sake. I don't think she had noticed Grandpa waiting in the car.

While Mrs Cunningham went into the house to get the drinks I looked rather severely at Pippy and told him firmly to stay, since he obviously intended to do that anyway. His tail thumped again and he laid his nose on his paws. Mrs Cunningham breezed out onto the terrace with a tray of tall glasses, each one containing not one or two ice cubes but six at least, as well as two straws. My drink was orange squash, but Grandma said afterwards she wasn't sure what hers was.

We sipped as quickly as we could, thinking of Grandpa, Lucy and our rapidly congealing dinner. Mrs Cunningham was explaining that Pippy seemed to have come into the garden from the woods at the back. "There is a fence but he must have tunnelled his way underneath or got through a hole or something. Jack Russells can get in anywhere, can't they? We used to have one ourselves, you see, so I know how they are. Your little Pip quite reminds me of Benjy, although Benjy had less brown on him. Where *is* Malcolm?"

Some conversation about the ways of Jack Russell terriers followed. Grandma finished her drink and said she thought it was time I put Pippy on his lead. He was feeling meek and chastened and grateful, like me, and put up no resistance. Grandma thanked Mrs Cunningham warmly, and at the front door our hostess bent down and shook Pippy's paw.

"No more running off for you, young puppy-dog!" she admonished.

We crossed the gravel to the car. Grandpa got out to open the door for us and raised his hat to Mrs Cunningham.

"Good-bye!" called Mrs Cunningham, waving. "Malcolm will be so sorry to have missed you!"

I let Pippy jump into the back of Lucy as usual and then straight away banished him to the floor, which is a tight space in a Morris Minor. It seemed unfair, because it wasn't his fault, but he must learn that running away did not pay, and in any case he was covered in dried mud. He remained on the floor all the way home, and over his head we discussed plans for his evening in stern and sorrowing voices. For his dinner menu, biscuits and thin gravy were decided upon, and the awful word "bath" was pronounced more than once, causing his ears to go so far back that I longed to give him a consoling pat. But in spite of everything I think he knew how glad we were to see him.

The next day we all went back to our usual selves. Pippy, being a wise dog as we have observed before, appeared to have forgotten the whole episode. I, on the other hand, being a wise child, would remember it for a long time.

Chapter Eleven
WEDNESDAY THE FIRST

September arrives – mysteries of the Manor House garden – undoubted benefits of decimalisation – half-day closing – departure of the house martins

THIS summer, like all the others before it, promised to go on for ever. But one day it was Wednesday September the First – and once September comes, however warm and sunny the weather may continue, nothing is quite the same.

I took the calendar off the kitchen wall, turned the page over to reveal a picture of the west front of Winchester Cathedral with fallen leaves strewn on the path, and felt the return of a familiar sensation. After all my yearning for an everlasting summer, here I was once again looking forward to seeing my friends, and thinking with positive relish of long socks, a new timetable, a new form teacher. It was strangely exciting to think that in just a few days Mum and I would be gathering everything together for school – buying new shoes (not a moment too soon) and hunting for my hockey stick and slide rule.

In that morning's post there was a letter from Mum saying they had bought some paint and wallpaper and were planning to spend the week-end sprucing up the kitchen. They had intended to come to Grandma's for Sunday lunch and stay the night, but because of the decorating they would come on Monday and take me back the same day, to leave time for last-minute shopping before school started.

In preparation for their arrival, a brand new cake of Pears soap would appear in the bathroom. Grandma would stick the old one to a green block of Fairy, to be used up in the kitchen. The end room would be made ready for tea, and I would pick some wall-flowers for the dining table. Then I would tidy away Grandma's knitting, the piles of papers from the settle and the other odds and ends around the house that you get rid of when visitors are coming.

But all that could wait. There were five whole days left before Mum and Dad's arrival, and one of those days was Saturday the Fourth, the day when Grandma and I were going to see the Manor House garden.

The Manor House is at the far end of the village, after the church and the shops, but before Water Lane and the allotments. Although it is a large house, only two people live in it – a husband and wife called Sir Raymond and Lady Short. They don't go back to the Domesday Book or anything like that. There hasn't been a Lord of the Manor in the village for well over a century. According to Grandpa, Sir Raymond is "one of these industry big-wigs". He bought the house to accommodate his five children, who have long ago grown up and left home.

The Manor House stands well back from the road, and in front of it there is a magnificent spreading tree. Grandma told me the name of the tree: Cedar of Lebanon. She said it might be two hundred years old.

The lawn it stands on is quite perfect: it always looks as if someone has just mown it, and the cedar casts dewy shadows across it on sunny mornings.

I once asked Grandma why there was never anyone sitting under the tree. I could clearly imagine a tea table there, with ladies in long white dresses holding frilly parasols, and a stiffly-bowing butler in attendance.

Grandma said it might not be very romantic to sit there in full view of the road, with passers-by looking at you. She believed there was a large walled garden behind the house, which would be much more private. I little thought that we would ever see that hidden garden.

But one day this summer, when I had been here about a week, I went into the Stores to spend my second lot of pocket money and noticed a poster stuck to the front of the Post Office counter in the corner. It was neatly hand-written in various colours of felt pen, and in the centre was glued a colour photograph of five young men leaning on a vintage car. They were all dressed alike in striped blazers and ties, white trousers and straw boaters, and three of them held musical instruments – a trumpet, a clarinet and a banjo. Across the top of the poster were the words, "JAZZ ON THE LAWN – BRING YOUR PICNIC." And at the bottom in smaller writing it said, "In the Manor House Garden. Saturday 4th September, 6pm. Adults 25p, Children 10p."

It still looked strange to see prices printed with "p" for "pence" instead of "d", and no more shillings, even though we'd been decimal since February, with plenty of time before that to get used to the idea – years of conversion sums at school, and shiny sets of coins in special wallets, and television adverts telling you how to work out your change.

Mrs Studley emerged from her inner sanctum behind the curtain and saw me reading the poster. "Do you think you might go to that, my love? Those lads really look something, don't they? That's Lady Short's grandson in the middle – the one with the trumpet. He's at one of the Oxford colleges and they've got a band there, and they're touring round the country all summer earning money to go to America, of all places, and Lady Short's letting them have the Manor House garden for one of their concerts. They're just as good as a grown-up band, she says. She gave me a pile of tickets to sell in the shop. Here they are, my love, if you want to buy some any time."

"I'll ask Grandma," I replied, and ran home without even buying my sweets. "Back in a minute!" I called to Old Tom as I shot past him.

Grandma thought it sounded very interesting, but she was sure Grandpa wouldn't want to come – too many people and the wrong sort of music. "He and the pup can keep each other company at home." She gave me an extra fifty-new-pence piece, and I ran straight back to the Stores with it. Once I had the tickets and Grandma's change safely in my pocket I could concentrate on the slightly less exciting, but still important, question of sherbet lemons.

Since September seemed a long way off then, I slid the concert tickets under a pot of china flowers on the chest of drawers in my bedroom, and didn't allow myself to look at them. But on Wednesday the First, as I turned the page of Grandma's kitchen calendar, the thought of school and of Mum and Dad coming gave way to the remembrance of those tickets, tucked away almost out of sight. I ran to fetch a pen, and was drawing a decorated ring round Saturday the Fourth when Grandma came in from the garden in her apron.

"I'll need some eggs if we're going to have a custard tart," she said. "Could you skip down to the farm some time this morning?"

"All right, Grandma." I went outside into the yard. There had been rain in the night, but the early sun was hot, and steam was rising off the concrete. It was a sparkling and beautiful morning. The milkman was late: two empty bottles still stood on the kitchen doorstep, with a note from Grandma sticking out from under one of them – "One extra gold-top today, please."

Pippy had been dozing against the fence in the sunshine, but sprang to life when he saw me. I decided to take him for a short walk, so as not to disappoint him, and then go to the farm for the eggs.

On the way up the lane I began explaining to Pippy that it would soon be time for me to go home. He was too busy nosing the banks to pay any attention, but I felt I was preparing him gently for my departure, all the same. I knew he would be all right. He would feel a bit lost just at first, but Grandma would sit down with him on her lap and explain everything. Then he would remember, and settle down quite happily to his other routine, without me here.

We wandered up the lane and back again slowly, so that Pippy could examine the banks in the required amount of detail. When we got home the milkman had delivered two pints of gold-top and one of silver, and there were already holes in the lids where the blue-tits had pecked through. Grandma must be busy – I could hear the vacuum cleaner whining upstairs. I took the bottles into the larder and replaced the wrecked tops with the rubber ones Mum had got for Grandma from our Betterware Man. Meanwhile Pippy had a drink from his bowl and settled down by the fence for a busy morning of paw-cleaning.

I looked in Grandma's purse for the egg money. In the purse was Grandma's ready-reckoner – a square of cardboard cut from a cereal packet, on the back of which she had written out a careful chart to help her understand the new money.

"1 new penny = 2 ½ d; 2 ½ new pence = 6d; 5 new pence = 1 shilling; 10 new pence = 2 shillings; 12 ½ new pence = half a crown; 50 new pence = ten shillings. 100 NEW PENCE TO THE POUND."

I can understand why Grandma and Grandpa find decimal money a bit of a struggle, although I'm delighted with it myself, because it makes maths questions at school so much easier. Grandpa says the new system is more sensible, but it takes some getting used to and he wishes the coins weren't so tiny. Grandma is determined to get the hang of the money, but she is sure she will never be able to think in metres or litres or grammes. Feet and inches, gallons and pints, pounds and ounces, will have to do, and fortunately Mr Ackland and Mrs Studley and even most of the shop-keepers in town agree with her. Sam is certainly not going to be selling his eggs in boxes of five and ten.

Down at the farm, I knocked on the kitchen door and waited until "Mrs Sam," as Grandma calls her, came out with her little boy Tony hanging onto her skirt. I asked for half a dozen eggs and she took the money and went back into the house for them.

Ned the collie was lying on the ridged concrete soaking up the morning sun,

with bits of straw clinging about his matted coat. The chickens clucked round the yard, making a contented little crooning sound in their throats. They placed their yellow feet most carefully as they turned this way and that, their heads bobbing with every step, picking up every stray wisp of anything that might be edible. The air smelt warmly of straw and manure.

The farmyard is a tatty place, and I often wonder why Sam doesn't tidy it up. He ought to sweep up all the mess and clear away the pieces of derelict machinery lying around in the corners. The barn could do with a nice new tiled roof instead of the rusty old corrugated iron one, but I suppose that would cost a lot of money. Grandpa says times are hard for farmers. He worries that Sam will sell out to a builder one of these days.

Mrs Sam brought the eggs out to me, bending over sideways so that Tony could help carry them. On my return home I counted twenty-seven swallows perched on the telephone wire over the lane.

I took Pippy with me into the garden, and we sat on the bench near the greenhouse listening to Sam's combine harvester going up and down the next field but one. I kissed the top of Pippy's sun-warmed head and told him again in my most matter-of-fact tone that I was going home soon. He licked my chin in return and gazed soulfully into my eyes with his paw on my arm, which I interpreted as a request to stay another few weeks.

"Now, Pippy," I replied, "I know perfectly well that Grandma is really your favourite person and you are going to have a very nice time here without me. Anyway, we'll see each other at Christmas when you come to my house."

I thought ahead to Monday. I was looking forward to seeing Mum and Dad again. Perhaps, like last year, I would be sitting in Grandma's arm-chair with Pippy asleep on my knee, and would hear our car crawling up the lane and pulling into the yard. They would get out of the car and close the doors quietly, as they always do, and I would put my fingers in

my ears ready for them to ring the doorbell and send Pippy yapping off my lap into the kitchen. Grandma's doorbell is very loud, and because the mechanism is on the kitchen wall, that's where it sounds the loudest. So when it rings, which isn't very often, Pippy hurtles in there, skidding on the lino, then realises that he has been fooled again and charges back to the front door where his guard-dog duty really lies.

Mum and Dad always ring the bell when they arrive, even though they could perfectly easily walk straight into the house by the kitchen door. They like to make a grand entrance, and anyway Mum can't resist making Pippy go through his doorbell routine.

Sitting by the greenhouse with Pippy, I made an effort to picture Mum and Dad in my mind. It was surprisingly hard, considering I had spoken to them on the phone quite recently. I could dimly picture Mum, slim and smart in her summer dress and red Scholl clogs, but I couldn't really visualise Dad at all, except for the regrettable moustache he grew last winter. (Who knows, he may have seen the light and shaved it off by Monday.)

The combine harvester droned on the distance, and Pippy got up and turned round and round on my lap to make himself more comfortable. We stayed there together until it was time to lay the table for mid-day dinner.

🕮

Grandma and I had planned to take Pippy for a long walk and pick some blackberries in the afternoon. But Grandma felt like a sit-down first, so I decided to put my wellingtons on and go to the stream while I waited. On my way through the orchard I found Grandpa reaching up into a tree with the long-handled apple-picker. A few wasps, or "apple-drains" as Old Tom calls them, buzzed around some fallen fruit in the grass. Grandpa pointed out a kestrel, circling above the wooded edge of Sam's barley field. He handed me the picker and I twisted off a dozen or so apples into the bag, until my arms were worn out with the effort. Then I waved him good-bye and went out through the back gate and down the lane.

Wednesday is half-day closing in the village, so there was no-one about, not even Old Tom. But further on as I passed the church, I saw one of the ladies who are on the cleaning rota kneeling in the church porch scrubbing the paving stones. It seemed friendly to go and join her, as we were the only two people about. I opened the gate and went up the steps into the churchyard. I thought her name was Mrs Vickery, but I wasn't quite sure, so I just said, "Hello."

"Hello, my dear," she replied, looking up as she dipped her scrubbing brush into a large bucket of frothy water. "That last brood of chicks are all flown now, so I'm cleaning up after them for good." She was talking about the house martins. They had glued their mud nest, like an upturned coconut shell, onto the inside wall of the porch a few feet above the door. All through the summer the cleaning ladies had had the job of scraping up the worst of the resulting mess from the paving stones so that the Sunday worshippers would not tread it into the church and ruin their best shoes into the bargain. Now it was time to restore the slabs to normal.

The church felt different on a weekday afternoon. Dark inside and empty of people, it seemed older and more remote than on a Sunday. On most Sunday mornings Grandma and I come to church for the service. I don't really understand it much, but I enjoy it – it is impressively solemn but friendly, and I like looking at the stained-glass windows and the carved pew ends, not one the same as another. If it's a hymn I know, I sing boldly, and if it's unfamiliar I quietly try to guess the tune as it goes along. I don't think Grandma goes to church much when I'm not here, but she always kneels by my bed at night, clasps her hands and closes her

eyes and says a prayer in her poetry-reading voice. Sometimes it's the Lord's Prayer, sometimes it's "Gentle Jesus".

Gentle Jesus, meek and mild,
Look upon thy little child.
Pity my simplicity,
Suffer me to come to thee.
Amen.

I watched Mrs Vickery give the scrubbing brush a final rinse and shake, carry the bucket of dirty water out into the road and empty it down the drain. After that I thought it would be polite to walk back with her as far as her front door.

I decided not to bother with the stream today after all. Grandma would be upstairs putting her face on by now, and the blackberries were waiting to join the apples in a pie.

Chapter Twelve
JAZZ ON THE LAWN

Milking the cows – peas and mint sauce – evening sunshine and a new kind of music – dusk falls – we dance in the rain – at home with Grandma

SOMETHING woke me early on Saturday the Fourth: perhaps it was the church clock, perhaps it was a cow. I climbed onto the window sill in my pyjamas and sat with my knees under my chin, catching the first oblique rays of sun. The sky was clear, but in my mind I could hear Grandpa saying, "Never trust a blue sky first thing in the morning".

More mooing floated up from the direction of the farm, and I realised I hadn't been down once this summer to watch the cows being milked. When I was small I used to go with Grandma quite often, not in the early morning but for the evening session. We would lean on the five-barred gate at the entrance to the farmyard, watching from a respectful distance while "the girls" waited in a patient overlapping queue for the milking machine, chewing the cud in their dreamy, rhythmic way and flicking away the flies with a flourish of the tail or a heavy shake of the head. Sam

never called any of them Daisy or Primrose, only "girl" or "old girl", but he spoke to them kindly and treated them gently. The metal tags in their ears always made me wince, but they didn't seem to mind them.

Eight cows at a time could go into the shed for milking. The milking machine had long pipes attached to it, and each pipe ended in a bunch of four rubber tubes which fixed onto a cow's udder. It made a *shunt-shunt-shunt* noise as it pumped the milk into tall silver churns. It was fun to watch, but Grandma sometimes said she felt sorry for the cows.

When milking was over the cows made their leisurely way out of the yard through the back gate, imprinting more hoof marks into the great delta of mud that spread out from the gate into the sloping field. To make ourselves useful we would open the main farmyard gate and hold it while Sam and his helper rolled the churns out into the lane on their bottom edge, swung them up onto their knees and heaved them onto the wooden shelf set into the bank, to be collected later by the milk lorry.

It was strange to think of this ritual still going on twice a day, every day, without our presence.

After a busy morning tidying up and running errands for Grandma and trying not to look at the steadily gathering clouds, I sat at the kitchen table shelling peas while Grandma peeled the potatoes for lunch. I pressed my thumb onto each pod until it split, then scraped out the peas, which were all attached to the inside of the pods by thin little stalks, and dropped them into the colander. The raw peas smelt so sweet I couldn't possibly resist eating some, especially the tiny ones which weren't worth cooking anyway. When they were all done I took the large bowl of empty pods out to the compost heap and handed my surprisingly meagre offering of peas to the cook.

If shelling peas is fun, making mint sauce certainly isn't. I picked a few sprigs from the mint bed outside the back kitchen door and held them to

my nose to make the most of their bewitching scent before I had to ruin it. Then, with a sigh, I began stripping the leaves off the stalks and stuffing them into the grinder. I wound the handle awkwardly round and round, and as usual ended up with a few mashed fragments of mint on the chopping board and the rest caught up in the works and needing to be tediously poked out with the point of a knife. What a shame, after all that effort, to mix the heavenly mint with sugar and most unheavenly vinegar! – but it must be done. Resignedly I stirred my little jug of thin liquid and tasted it. As always, the flavour of vinegar had won hands down. Grandpa came in from changing out of his gardening clothes and said, "Ooh! Mint sauce!" and I went into the living room to lay the table.

During dinner Pippy the Dog Who Knows His Place was shut in the kitchen. The rich aroma of roast lamb must have been knocking his nose off, but he would have to wait patiently for his dinner until we had all finished ours. It would be worth waiting for. Grandpa would take all the rest of the meat off the joint and sort out the scrappiest pieces as he went along, putting them in Pippy's bowl with his biscuits and gravy ("something for the inner dog"). Grandma would then secretly add a few select morsels which Grandpa had been keeping for his own next meal, and after thoroughly polishing his dish Pippy would conclude his feast by taking the bone outside.

To my great disappointment, when I went to let him out I saw that the sky had now clouded up completely, and by the time the washing up was finished he was sitting on the doorstep in a fine misty drizzle, waiting to come in and hoping that his bone would be admitted as well.

What if Jazz on the Lawn had to be cancelled after all the waiting? Even if it went ahead as planned, jazz on a damp lawn didn't seem quite so delightfully summery.

But Grandma was undismayed. She said that a fine morning often means a fine evening, whatever happens in between, and we could take a polythene sheet to put under our picnic rug. As she had predicted, by the time we set off down the lane with our picnic things the sun had been

out for some time, and the clouds had moved so far off we didn't even bother to take umbrellas.

As we walked in through the open gates and along the Manor House drive, I shivered with anticipation. For a moment I had been shocked to see the idolised front lawn covered with parked cars and churned into mud in places, but I quickly decided there was no point in worrying – the organisers must know what they were doing. Music was floating on the air from somewhere, and along past the corner of the house we saw an open door in the stone wall, where two men in linen jackets and straw hats stood next to a small table. We joined the queue of people who were waiting to go in, and the older of the two men raised his hat to us and said "Good evening, ladies." The younger one took our tickets, remarking what a good thing it was that the weather had bucked up.

We filed through the door, and there spread before our privileged eyes was the secret garden in evening splendour. On three sides of the garden, protected from wind by the high wall, were borders filled with ornamental shrubs, and red, gold, purple and white flowers, and on the fourth side there were glasshouses built against the wall, brightly reflecting the late sun. Everywhere there were groups of people reclining on rugs or sitting on folding chairs or walking about looking for a place to settle down. They added up to a considerable crowd, and there were still more people coming in behind us through the door in the wall. The concert must have been advertised in other places beside our Post Office Stores.

It wasn't quite six o'clock yet, but the jazz band was already playing in a relaxed sort of way under a white canopy, the young men dressed in straw boaters and striped blazers just as they had been on the poster. Their music was attached to the music stands with clothes-pegs to stop a gust of wind blowing it away. One of them played the clarinet, one the drums, one the double bass and one the banjo. The fifth, who must be Lady Short's grandson, held a trumpet casually by his side and surveyed the audience, tapping the beat with his foot and exchanging occasional remarks with the rest of the band.

Scanning the crowd, we couldn't see many familiar faces, but Grandma spotted Fred and Olive Parrish who live at the Old Cider House opposite the Post Office Stores, so we spread out our ground-sheet and picnic rug in a space next to them. Grandpa always asks "Old Parrish", who knows a thing or two about fruit trees, to help him when he prunes the trees in the orchard.

Gazing round me while the music played and the last members of the audience took their places, I thought this was the most beautiful garden I had ever been in. The plants looked comfortable against the old stone wall, the frames of the glasshouses were freshly painted, and the garden was altogether so tranquil and perfect I could understand very well why no-one ever sat on the front lawn under the spreading cedar tree.

The leader of the band gave the others several slow nods and then raised his trumpet to his lips: the concert had officially begun.

This Jazz on the Lawn was not a bit like the sort of musical events I sometimes go to with Mum and Dad. At serious concerts in concert-halls you have to sit stock still, almost holding your breath so as not to make a sound. I do enjoy those concerts, but it is hard work keeping quiet, and you have to be very careful not to clap at the wrong time. Here, on the other hand, it seemed to be quite acceptable to talk and laugh during the music. The band members chatted to each other when it wasn't their turn to play. People burst into enthusiastic applause whenever one of them played a solo; sometimes they even shouted out and whooped. Several small children were playing about among the audience, and from time to time trying out handstands and cartwheels on the damp grass.

The tunes had names like "Ain't misbehavin'" and "It don't mean a thing". They were songs I had never heard before, but Grandma seemed to know most of them. They really made you feel like dancing, yet except for the cartwheeling children, no-one did. It seemed that everyone was too shy to stand up and be the first. Whenever the trumpeter, who was also the main singer, announced another piece and urged us all to dance, most people just looked at each other and pulled sheepish faces, and

even the bravest only jiggled about half-heartedly while still sitting down. "It's being British that does it," said Grandma. "We're hopeless."

In the first half of the concert we ate our sandwiches, pork pie and hard-boiled eggs, and drank tea from our thermos flask. Then there was an interval, during which people walked round the garden and admired it, and Grandma chatted to Mr and Mrs Parrish. I wandered off by myself, in and out of the lengthening shadows, to look at the glasshouses and marvel at the ruler-straight rows of pots along the shelves, all placed at precisely the same distance apart. On my way back I saw Mrs Studley with her Jim pointing out something in one of the flower borders, but I felt too shy to go and say hello – she looked different without her overall.

The musicians, having put down their instruments for the interval, went and stood at one end of the lawn in the sun, and people clustered round to listen while they sang unaccompanied barbershop songs. At the beginning of each song Lady Short's grandson hit his hat with a tuning fork, which made everyone laugh. The close harmony sounded clear and rich, the voices perfectly in tune. After four or five songs they sauntered back with their hands in their pockets to start the jazz again. I thought the clarinet player was the handsomest. The drummer had the longest hair.

As the second half got under way the sun finally dropped out of sight. Lanterns had been lit in the flower borders and the coloured lights draped on a wire round the canopy shone encouragingly, but the garden was beginning to grow cold. Grandma and I pulled our coats round us, moved closer together and slowly sipped the remains of the tea from the flask, using the cups to warm our hands and our hands to warm the cups.

After a while, the concert seemed to be dragging just a little. There were longer and longer pauses between the pieces, while the band sorted through piles of music and discussed what they were going to play next. A chilly breeze had sprung up, and a few families with small children were beginning to pack up and go, tiptoeing away with apologies. Then Lady Short strode over during one of the pauses and had a word with her grandson, and Grandma whispered in my ear, "I think she's telling him

it's time they finished." There was a brief conference under the canopy, after which the trumpeter came forward and announced that the next piece was the last, and would be the highlight of the evening. Despite this promise people were still gathering up their belongings and leaving in twos and threes, bowing and smiling to the band as they went. It was growing quite gloomy, and I wondered how the players could see their music.

I looked up at the darkening sky and felt spots of rain. Mrs Parrish put her coat over her head to stop the rain spoiling her perm, and Mr Parrish raised his hat and wished us goodnight. With rapid efficiency he picked up all their gear and they scuttled away. Most of the other members of the audience were also hastily folding rugs and chairs, and some hoisted umbrellas.

"Sorry I left the brollies at home," said Grandma. "We don't want to miss the end, do we? Let's just get wet."

But we didn't get wet, because just then something happened to change everything. The trumpeter stepped from beneath the awning and called out with a grand gesture of welcome, "It's dry under here – why don't you come and join us?"

Without waiting for a second invitation, the scattered remains of the audience began to gather close around the band as it struck up its long-awaited finale, and there, sheltered from the rain and wrapped in the soft gleam of the coloured lights, we all began to dance at last. Grandma did the waltz with me as a partner, then twirled gently by herself for a while, then just laughed. In the darkness beyond the canopy, through a curtain of falling rain, you could see large and small umbrellas swaying and bobbing as the few people still left outside began dancing as well, and not only dancing but singing along to the chorus and clapping the beat. It was so pally I felt sorry Grandpa was missing it, although I couldn't really imagine how he would fit in.

The joyful music in the glowing pool of light made me wave my arms and stamp and sing and grin from ear to ear. I wanted it never to end. But eventually there had to be a chorus which slowed down and stopped

instead of turning into yet another. Everyone clapped and shouted "More, more! Encore!", but Lady Short said it really was time to finish, as there was still everything to clear away – and Lady Short's voice had a ring of authority. So we all said Good-bye and Thank You to the band and to people in general, and processed obediently out of the garden in a murmur of surrounding chatter, humming to ourselves and beaming at strangers as though they were our family.

Grandma and I didn't feel the least bit cold any more. We danced all the way home, laden though we were with our rug and groundsheet and picnic basket, humming the last chorus over and over and enjoying the cool specks of drizzle on our faces.

Back at the house, Grandpa was asleep by the fire – having a "ziz" as he would call it – with Pippy stretched out at his feet. *Far from the Madding Crowd* lay open upside down on the arm of the chair. Pippy must have had his evening walk: he barely raised his head as we came in.

We sat down in our places in the inglenook, and our faces glowed in the firelight. I rubbed my hands together, right over left, left over right – the gentle rain had made them softer than they had ever been in my whole life.

"Did you ever go to concerts when you were a girl, Grandma?"

"Well, let me think. There were good bands at the dance hall and the ice rink. And we used to go to our cousins' house sometimes – they used to roll back the carpet and dance to a gramophone. That was fun. But I can't remember ever going to what you might call a concert in those days. Going to the pictures was what we did then – the whole family together. We went by bus and queued up outside for ages. They were silent films then. My Auntie Lil played the piano accompaniment sometimes."

I had seen some of those old silent films on television, so I knew what they were like.

"Did she have to play very fast when there was a chase or something?"

"Yes, and dreamily in the romantic part. She was very clever at it. We always had fish and chips afterwards and got the last bus home. If we

missed the bus we had to walk. We were pretty late to bed some Saturday nights. Speaking of which, we don't want dark circles under those eyes when your Mum and Dad come on Monday."

I sighed and stood up. "I won't be able to sleep."

"Just read for a while. You'll soon nod off. I'll be up to say goodnight in a few minutes."

Grandpa was still fast asleep. I kissed the top of his head and danced up to bed, tapping out jazz rhythms on the sixteenth-century stairs.

Sunday evening, 5th September

Mum and Dad rang an hour ago, to say that the kitchen is now lime green with a geometric-patterned feature wall and they will be here by eleven tomorrow. My summer at Grandma's is nearly over, after all, but my typewriter has recorded everything. I haven't let anybody read it yet, but one day I will.

Outside in the dusk it's raining, and just cold enough for a fire. Grandma is knitting on her stool, I am on my log and Grandpa is in the kitchen making tea. Pippy the Dog is snoring.

Tomorrow is still a long way off. Just for now, Grandma and I will stay sitting in the inglenook, one each side of the hearth. We'll talk of this and that, and when there's nothing left to say we'll be silent, listening to the whispering fire and the slow tick of the clock in the hall.

To the knoll
Sam's field
The back gate
To the village